Exit of a Dragonfly

Exit of a Dragonfly

— An Odyssey —

by

Neville Shulman

BRECHINSET PUBLICATIONS
7-11 King Street, Ipswich, Suffolk, England IP1 1EG.

ISBN 0–947681–40–X

Designed and typeset by Brechinset, Ipswich, Suffolk
Printed and Bound by The Garden City Press Limited, Letchworth

Contents

Chapters

Contents

Emma Alon
Lee Lauren
and
Dragonfly

Minus One

My name is Exit. It's not my original, of course, but one I adopted many years ago. There is no other I would now answer to or even recognise. I don't get any calls, I don't receive letters.

I don't have or use a first name, and it's easy to pass through life without one. Many people use one name only and thereby create a formality which prevents unwelcome intrusion and intimacy which is obtained by an immediate use of someone's first name. Sometimes I have to use initials and these vary depending upon my mood and my humour. T is my favourite. One of the questions most asked is "Where is The Exit?" and if pressed, I can always say the T stands for Theo. TO Exit is one of my secret jokes. Sometimes I use N with the O, standing for NO Exit. If I have anything to say about my final epitaph I will choose 'Exit Left'.

Exit is a word I have always loved. In use everywhere, prominent, yet unobtrusive, so active and yet passive, used without any real consideration of its meaning or origin. From the Latin exere, to go out, Exit means he, she or it, goes out. Even those taught Latin do not seem to be conscious of the real meaning of the word, merely accepting it as a direction or a sign, a word from a dead language kept alive by its own power. But then most people are unaware, blindly unaware of most things. How many see that fiery ball suspended and motionless in the sky? Suppose the Sun were To Exit. . .

Right from our very beginnings recognition has been sought after. We all want our names in print or up in lights, and wherever I go — theatres, cinemas, trains or planes — there it is, shining out of the dark, commanding, brightly lit, necessary.

When I am low this secret, this identity I've created, is my personal comforter.

I was low now, very low, and very, very unhappy, on a flight going east and I didn't care whether it was going west, as long as it was over soon. The aeroplane was crowded to capacity with aggravated and aggravating people, hot, shiny and very impatient. I had been given one of the few remaining seats, twenty minutes before it was supposed to take off, and I had thought my luck was in. But my luck was out. Definitely out. I was jammed between two people who were not going to allow me to journey in peace. To my right was a large overflowing lady, probably in her thirties, but with sixty years of excess that she could not stow away and I was the beneficiary of her largesse. She was very excitable, with expansive arm movements that had captured over a third of my seat as well as holding on to her own territory. Within half an hour of taking off there were four or five wrestling contests, and to use an obvious phrase, I was losing hands down. On my left was a thin man, thin that is, in comparison to my other neighbour. He was wearing a pair of very serious horn-rimmed pebble glasses that continually bounced light and reflection, so that his slightest movement caused him to appear to sway menacingly in every direction. Added to this he possessed some long curved and ornate weapon which I supposed was a pipe, although to my knowledge he neither actually smoked it nor sucked on it. But he made good use of it, waving it and tapping it, first in one hand, then in the other. I received one or two fierce jabs right at the beginning which caused me to concede more of my seat to him as well, and from then on I kept trying to shrink into a central position which would enable me to survive. What an omen of thought that turned out to be.

At least two of my comforters were there, to the left and to the right, shining brightly, the etched lettering giving me some strength as I prepared to wait painfully for the flight to end. I tried to watch the film, just to pass some of the time, but it did not make much sense. Some of it was out of synchronisation, inaudible and I presumed that parts had been cut for family consumption which helped to make it more incomprehensible. Of course, there was the possibility that the film would have been less understandable with those parts kept in, but that really was too difficult a thought to deal with, so I concentrated on keeping myself in the centre of my seat, as much out of harm's way as possible.

It was unbearably hot, everyone and everywhere the same; there was no escape. I thought about stretching my legs in the narrow gangways, but I really did not have the strength to go through an encounter either to my right or left. If the going out could be accomplished without much pain there would still be the coming back, and I would certainly be made to suffer. As if reading my mind, a quick squashing came from the right and a sharp jab from the left which decided me to stay where I was. I tried to sleep or just doze, but it was impossible in the position I was in — my legs and back stiff and rigid — I could find no way of sitting that would allow me a measure of comfort even for a short while.

God popped into my mind.

I had not invited Him, not consciously anyhow. Whenever I am in a plane I am liable to think about Him more than at other times. Probably most people are the same. It might be something to do with the idea that God resides up in the heavens and therefore when flying you must be getting closer to Him and are more likely to be invited in for tea, so to speak. Of course, in an aeroplane you are something of a captive audience. Perhaps on future flights we will all end up watching or listening to religious commercials.

Then God popped out.

The lights had been turned off in the cabins and everyone was trying to sleep. Even my volatile companions were no longer so active and I was getting into a Quasimodo position which was becoming almost tolerable. The Exit lights still shone of course and they gave enough light to reveal the rows of silhouettes that sat shoulder to shoulder all the way down, in the dimness

11

looking like rows of fairground coconuts with fuzzy wigs askew. Then my name started to go out. First the left, then the right. Then both came on again, then both went out. Possibly I was the only one to notice, but it was important to me. "Put my name back on!" I wanted to scream; then someone did scream. The engine noise had changed, and while I had been worrying about the Exit lights, someone had noticed the change. There was no steady drone, but a high pitched whine which quickly developed into an ear piercing screech, and every light flashed on; NO SMOKING, FASTEN SEAT BELTS, EXIT, EXIT. . . and then they all went out — and stayed out, and it was very dark. Everyone was awake and grabbing at seat belts, but I was five seconds in advance of them. The plane nose-dived and we were all forced forward against the backs of the seats in front, except for those right at the front who were sent sprawling, their cries the loudest. The air was filled with screams, cries, moans, and a terrible fear. Then the fear swallowed up all the rest. It ran up and down the gangways, swelling with every second, the only freely moving object (or was it the subject?), its shape becoming enormous and all powerful.

Over the intercom. came a girl's voice, sweet and soft, "Stay calm, fasten your . . ." then her own nerve gave way, perhaps she had seen the fear monster, and she screamed in terror, her voice ugly and harsh. The intercom was cut, but we could still hear her scream under its own volition, running unchecked, frantically seeking some easy release. Then the plane rolled to the right and I was thrown on top of the fat woman, pressed into her huge soft thighs, and my hands made contact with a massive breast. Some crazed joke about living off the fat of the land pierced my mind but it was quickly crowded out by total hysteria followed by total fear. The woman underneath me did not cry out. Her voice had tried to escape first, on its own, and had died in the attempt, but I could feel her wriggling beneath me as if trying to move her great weight into an upright position. She was wearing clothes, but it was as though she was not and I wondered if she was thinking she had a naked man lying on top of her, or if that was the last thought that would enter her mind. Whatever it was it became her last thought. The fear of crashing was so terrible that the crash itself was almost welcome as a final resolution. There wasn't one single noise of the crash, but a staccato series of sounds as if the plane was bouncing on its nose before coming to rest. Screams started off separately in more than a hundred different throats and then rose in unison to become a crescendo, crowding out everything else and then being drowned by the blackness which swept in and took command. My last thought was whether the pilot would or should allow this, but that became his worry; mine was to fight off the cobra that had seized my throat and was trying to choke my life away.

First

I was having a marvellous dream. I did not want to wake from it. I was lying on an enormous waterbed, eating deliciously soft and creamy marshmallows. I felt that I had slept really deeply and well. I could feel the sun shining directly on me, warming and welcoming. I awoke slowly — and then I knew that death was all around me. I did not need to see it, neither did I want to see it.

I was still lying on top of the fat woman. She was still very fat, but now she was very dead as well. How I had been saved, why I was not also dead, I could not begin to understand. I eased myself off her, slowly and timidly, as if she might awake at any moment and accuse me of rape. It has been said that rape is a fate worse than death, but given the choice I do not think the fat woman would have agreed. Somehow it seemed as if I had both violated her and taken her life away. She had lost out twice. The aircraft was in pieces and so were most of the passengers. The carnage was terrible, I could not take it in, so I tried to look away, but where was there to look? Don't let it penetrate into my brain, keep my gaze downwards, try to create blinkers that allow no chink of side vision. I tried to stand upright, and was amazed to be able to do so. Surely something in me, of me, must be destroyed, broken or at least damaged. I could not live and they could not die without there being some connection, some injury, which would not make me a leper amongst the dead. My clothes had been torn into shreds and I realised I had neither shoes nor socks on. Of course, I had taken my shoes off before the crash, but how did my socks disappear?

Was I really alive? A large bird flew silently by paying no attention to me or the remnants around me. There was still life somewhere. Was I to try and rejoin it? My head started to throb, raising my hand to my temple I felt a piece of torn flesh, my fingers touched a patch of drying blood. Yes, I had been hurt! I felt some strange relief at that knowledge. My head started to throb even more, my vision blurred and my eyes were going in and out of focus. I sank to my knees and the blinkers fell off and I saw the twisted bodies lying around, their tragic faces registering their disbelief. I had no control of my sight or my mind. When my vision cleared the bodies became a blur and when my vision blurred the image of the bodies appeared in stark relief, with the flesh falling away until I could see only their skeletons. I had no idea of time or how long we had been here. The fat woman was still fat, dead fat; her skeleton would be a long time coming. I started to pick my way out of the wreckage, still trying to avoid eye contact and to ignore the twisted and smashed bodies, but they were not to be ignored, they would force themselves into my path, until I recoiled and tried to step in another direction. Fortunately it did not take many steps before I was free of the bodies, and the strewn parts of the wreckage diminished and vanished very quickly as I staggered away.

I did not look back. I was in a desert; at least there was sand all around, and even to the horizon all I could see were sand dunes with clumps of bushes and a few small trees. I walked on.

For some reason I wanted to laugh, and then I actually did, a harsh unfeeling laugh, the first sound I had heard since the crash. Some distance away was a signpost which I crazily thought would contain the announcement of the next plane that would take off after the remains of this one had been swept away. It took quite an effort to make my way slowly towards it, my feet sinking heavily into the sand. The sign looked brand new, clean and upright, but there was nothing on it; I could not tell if it had always been like that or if it had been wiped clean by the wind or something else. It was pointing somewhere, but telling me to go nowhere; loose within its hole,

I found I could point it in any direction. I presumed this meant I could walk in any direction I wanted, but I did not want to go anywhere neither did I know where to go. I twirled it once and it pointed back to where I had come from and for the first time I turned round. I was now some way from the wreckage which I could see in its entirety, creating some strange symmetry in the way it had fallen. The nose cone was buried downwards into the sand and most of the wreckage had broken off and opened into a large number of pieces that had been flattened yet were still part of the main shape of the aeroplane, heading towards the tail which was pointing upwards in contrast to the nose cone. The desert was quickly trying to reclaim its territory and already everything was being covered with layers of fine sand. Covered in this way the bodies seemed less hideous and less obvious, some even appearing as if they were sunbathing or sheltering from the sun on some bizarre holiday outing.

Why should I be the only one still alive? There might be others! Why didn't I think of that before? Weakly, I started to run towards the wreckage, stumbled, fell over, got up and kept running and stumbling towards it. I rushed from body to body but my hope was in vain, no one else had survived. For the first time I cried. I sank upon my knees, the tears rolling down towards the sand, at least one drop hitting it for each dead person. The bird I had seen before again flew by, but this time with a companion, they seemed to be waiting for me to move on so they could carry out their own survey. They weren't vultures, merely investigators. The thought came that perhaps I should bury the dead but it seemed too major an undertaking and I decided to let the desert bury them. I had no idea where I was. I would have to try and get somewhere — to some kind of civilisation. But this was my civilisation, this wreckage, this dead plane and these dead bodies.

My head was hurting again, probably I was going to die as well; was dead; had gone crazy, or would go crazy. My mind felt as if it would burst at any moment. What had I been saved for?

Some special purpose? Funny that: the thought seemed to stir a childhood memory, of a time when I had felt really special, and had subsequently realised that all children felt that way until a sufficient number of disappointments had driven nails into the dreams, until they ceased to fly. I had just flown, and the nails were all around me. I could have died here, but I didn't, and I knew I couldn't give up now, that I must start the journey, my own Odyssey, to wherever it would lead, even if the end was no better than the beginning.

I felt as if I were ransacking a graveyard as I took from the wreckage some items I might need and put them into a canvas bag I strapped onto my back. I had to leave many things behind as I dared not overload the bag, neither did I know for how long I would have to journey before I reached somewhere, anywhere. I found sandals and clothes that more or less fitted and took one extra set in case room-service, or desert-service, was not available. Was I already going mad? I raised my hand to my head and felt the scarred tissue and immediately the throbbing started again. I took my hand away and it stopped.

I saw a piece of broken mirror, picked it up and stared at the face which looked back without acknowledgement or recognition. A man much older than myself, unsmiling, hollowed, haunted eyes, bloodied torn forehead. I threw the piece of mirror away and it twisted in the air; the sun struck it and suddenly I saw in it the plane at the airport, people secure and happy, climbing into it, and there was the younger me, standing at the top, waving, and for a moment I could not stop myself raising a hand and waving back. Then the mirror fell, and with it my foolishness and the memory.

I did not stop until I had reached the next hill and had laboriously climbed over it. I did not look back once.

Blue

It was another day. I had to keep going, trying to walk in a straight line heading for the mountain in the distance. My legs could not keep up this effort for long and stops became more frequent as the sun continued its climb overhead. There was no shade and often the throbbing in my head became so unbearable that I would have to stop and lie down until it had eased.

I was feeling really unwell; unhappy, depressed, full of pain. I did not know where I was going, except forward, to the mountains. I wanted to stop, but I had nothing to stop for. By evening, when the sun disappeared, the light grew grey and dull, then black, full of gloom, full of aggression. The ground became soft and gave way under my feet, as if trying to suck them down, not wanting to let them go, so each step became a greater effort than the last, sluggish and laboured.

From the empty landscape, I crossed a rise and was surrounded by blackened and burnt trees — dying or lifeless — twisted into shapes of despair. Their branches snatched at my face, they became thicker and more twisted, until I had to fight my way through them. The ground felt rubbery and yielding, the tangled undergrowth threatening to pull me down. The scene was nightmarish and, as I staggered on, I started to cry. Part of me was almost uncaring about what was happening, yet perversely I managed to struggle on.

Then I was crying quite openly, hardly conscious of my surroundings, just the necessity to continue. My heart was pounding and my head felt like bursting, then without warning I came into a clearing where I paused to gather my strength and to decide what I could do. I heard the roar of an aeroplane and looked up with hope. Then I saw it, flying low overhead, massive and out of control, and knew immediately that it was the plane in which I had been travelling.

Of course I knew what would happen before it did, but I also knew that there was no way to prevent it. The aircraft started to dive, screeching through the air, its wings seeming to float backwards as if made of soft material. The whole plane changed from a hard, solid object into a soft, uncontrolled one which floated outwards in all directions into obscene shapes. The nose started to head downwards and even before it hit the ground it collapsed as if on impact. As it struck all noise disappeared. There was utter silence, and the plane disintegrated into a slow-motion dance of destruction, its parts bouncing in all directions. I heard a scream, but it was quickly cut off and there was total silence again. The scream was repeated and again cut off. The plane was a thousand pieces of twisted metal scattered at random, but instead of corpses, dummies lay mis-shapen in the wreckage as if placed by some cruel hand to resemble lifeless bodies, without thought and strangely even without death. They just did not exist.

I jumped with pain throwing myself at the sky but instead of falling, I felt myself rise and float over the wreckage, arms and legs spreadeagled, helpless, as if given a special punishment of being made to witness the tragedy and death spread out in front of me. I could take no more and fell to the ground which rushed upwards to welcome me as I sank into its oblivion.

Tears woke me. I felt as if I was drowning as they ran into my mouth, their wetness sticky like blood, blood mixed with water. I lay on my face. I could not raise myself but managed to roll over onto my back. At first my eyes were sightless, then they were able to focus on a book which was being carried effortlessly along in the air, just slightly tossed and buffeted. The pages of the book fell out, one by one, fluttering downwards and out of sight, until all that was left was the black outer cover; then that was swept upwards and upwards, becoming a tiny black speck until it vanished altogether.

I felt I could not remain here and managed painfully to pick myself up. I stood unsteadily on my feet until some strength returned and I could continue my way to the mountain which was the only goal I knew and I had to retain if I was not to drift aimlessly in all directions. That I knew would be fatal. I must go on.

It took less time to reach the mountain than I had expected although my mind floated in and out of consciousness and I had no idea how long I had been walking. I started to climb.

Every part of the mountain was thick with grey ash. Each footstep caused the ash to swirl, to dance and rise so that shortly I was covered with it. It forced its way into my eyes, nostrils and ears, so that I had to stagger on, blinded and choked, unable even to hear my own footsteps. I tried to walk more slowly to lessen the movement but the ash continued to rise and I felt as if I would drown. It blotted out every sense, infiltrating into my very mind as if trying to destroy my reason. I thought I might go mad — or perhaps had already gone mad. I tried to concentrate only on the path ahead, but my mind would conjure up images of decaying flowers, infested fruit and flocks of wild-eyed birds that suddenly appeared in their thousands to dive into the earth and ocean. I could not think in a logical way, so I staggered on like a crazed bull elephant that had been shot but refused to lie down and enter the kingdom of its ancestors.

The rains came as suddenly as an erotic thought, and so fiercely that they seemed to have existed forever. Within moments the battle was at an end, the ash surrendered its supremacy and power, vanishing beneath a force of water that swept everything before it. I too surrendered quickly and was beaten to my knees, then forced down further and made to lie flat as the rain crashed down trying to cascade everything before it. I had almost drowned before in the ash, now I was drowning again. Face down, unable to move, I was crucified a thousand times as nails of water hammered me into the earth forcing me to create my own impression beneath me. The water covered me almost completely, only by turning my mouth downhill was I able to make a pocket of air and continue to breathe, just. Then the rain stopped but it was some time before I realised it because the pain was so great. My face and body slowly came alive, alive with a hundred pains from the cuts caused by stones that had struck me before being swept on past me to the valley below.

Making a great and painful effort I rolled over onto my back. Overhead a vulture hovered, waiting for me to die before making its descent. As our eyes locked, the bird screeched out as it realised I had cheated it, for now, and it circled away to look for another more immediate victim. On all fours, feeling like a mad dog, I scrambled upwards to the summit. There was a hollow, full of water, into which I crawled to soak away some of the blood and pain. I lay in the water so that it washed over my face, just raising my nose and lips occasionally to breathe. I fell asleep. When I awoke I was on my back and there was no water and I could not move as I had sunk into the ground so that only my eyes, nose and mouth seemed to be above it. I was able to squint downwards and see that grass covered every part of the ground where my body should be and I could see ants and other insects moving through it, nonchalantly, unafraid and seemingly unaware of my presence. I could not feel my body, my arms or legs, or indeed any part of myself. I tried to see my nose but it was too close and just looked like a small mound that protruded out of the earth. I tried to whistle, to create some sound, but all I could hear was the wind blowing through the grass.

Gradually my eyes tired, the lids closed and the dust spread over them mingling with the ground, and then there was no need to open my eyes again.

Four

My head throbbed and ached. My legs also ached continually; in fact not one part of me did not ache, and in thinking about it my head began to throb even more so I tried to ignore the pain by just concentrating on keeping one foot moving slowly in front of the other.

The landscape was grey, dark and miserable, I gained no inspiration from it as I passed through it, feeling only its oppressiveness. I longed for a soft bed with clean and comforting sheets. That thought made me drowsy and in the gathering dusk I missed my footing, stumbled and almost fell. I kept my head down, not wanting to see how far I had to go, trying to avoid the realisation, when I knew, that what was ahead was merely a repetition of the landscape I was going through now, stretching far into the distance, the same monotonous and overcast land.

Eventually I did raise my head slightly, and saw a light shining, almost beckoning, ahead to the right. I immediately made my way towards it, treating it as some kind of marker towards which I could strive and keep myself moving at a faster pace. The shaft of light came through the darkness towards me, its beam occasionally broken by night creatures that flew through it, mostly silent, but a few emitting a slight cry. As I neared the light source I could see it came from an enormous baronial house which was in total darkness except for one window from which came the beam of light. I approached the house realising as my footsteps crunched and echoed that the ground in front of it was covered in gravel. The beam of light was immediately switched off as if it had taken fright and the whole house was plunged into darkness, standing abandoned and forlorn, as if unoccupied. But someone must have switched off the light. For a moment I stood still, nonplussed at this reaction to my presence, but I decided to enter and find whoever was there.

The door had neither knocker nor bell or any visible means of attracting attention. Somehow I was reluctant to hammer upon it and I was about to try and see if there was an approach from another side when the door opened. It did not creak or give out any sound but swung smoothly as if suddenly admitting defeat. I hesitated for only a moment before entering. I passed through the doorway and found myself in a small lobby without any corridors or doors leading from it. The only way to continue was by one of four staircases leading upwards. I chose the one furthest to my right and followed it upwards as it curved in a semi-circle around and above. It led to a small landing on which there was only one door. I opened it and entered a room which was richly furnished with heavy drapes and brocades, several armchairs and an elegant chaise longue. In the middle of the floor stood a large square fish tank. The water was dank, slimed green and at first impenetrable, but after peering down into it for a while gradually I was able to see that it was in fact full of movement and I caught glimpses of goldfish and other fish swimming around. I gently touched the tank and immediately it cracked, splitting in two, so that all the water rushed out and the fish fell gasping upon the floor. Full of anguish I recoiled in horror, then desperately wanted to help but could see no means of rescuing them and I turned away in order not to see their last agonies. I tried to leave the room but now saw there were two doors, side by side, and I could not decide by which I had entered. I chose one, opened it and went through and came out onto a landing which was not the same one from which I had entered as there was a staircase again leading upwards, and none leading downwards. I climbed it and it led to another room. I entered and in the centre was a long wooden table around which sat eight people in sombre attire, with downcast, mournful, faces. They did not speak, but focused their attention on me as soon as I entered and stared seriously and sadly at me. Then

23

all together they rose and in single file walked past me in order to leave the room, still without a word, and without changing their expressions. I decided to follow but the door was shut and I heard a key turning from the outside. There was no handle on the inside and I could not see a keyhole.

I fumbled with the door but could not shift it, it looked as if it had been shut permanently and I felt I would not be leaving through it. However, there was a window. I walked to it and drew back the curtains which crumbled in my hands into thousands of mouldering pieces falling to the floor. The dust rose up and momentarily blinded me. As my sight returned I saw that the window was heavily barred, with iron bars deeply rusted and pitted from years of neglect. In one corner there was a large oak cupboard and hoping to find something to help my escape I went to it, opened it and quickly saw it was filled with hundreds of books, files and papers, each one bearing my name, or my photograph, referring to some part of my life, or the lives of people I had known. There was even a photograph of this house. The room was becoming very oppressive with the air full of thick dust and I was finding it difficult to breathe. I knew I could die here, surrounded by these records of my past life, and I had to make an effort to break free before my strength was drained away. I dragged the table to the door and tried to use it to batter it down but it was too heavy to lift and the door was too strong and I just stirred up further clouds of dust to choke me.

The window was the only possibility and in desperation I grasped the bars and pulled furiously at them. They came away so suddenly and easily that I fell backwards still clutching them. I landed in a heap on the floor with the bars lying on top of me. Momentarily I was stunned, and then struggled to my feet and saw that the bars had rusted away from the wood in which they had been fixed and the whole of the frame around the window had collapsed and disintegrated. The glass of the window shattered as soon as I touched it and I gulped at the clean air that swept in. I knocked out the remaining pieces of glass and then climbed on to the window sill and peered down. It was very high and I could see nothing which would help me lower myself. I felt more frightened of what was in the room and behind me, than what was outside and below, so bending myself forward I launched myself downwards. I hit the gravel with a tremendous thud, my legs seemed to snap under both my weight and the force, and two agonising pains shot up from each ankle through my legs as I rolled over screaming and screaming, until I knew no more.

I awoke and it was very bright. I was in a room which was completely white, several lights blazed down on me. I tried to raise my arms but they were pinned or tied to my side, and I could only half raise my head in order to look around. The bed was huge, very neat and tidy, and I felt very small within it. The blankets had been tucked in tightly on either side and were very flat to the bed. I could not see any shapes that would be made by the pressure of my legs. I tried to wriggle my toes and move my legs but there was no reaction. The door opened and someone entered carrying a pair of shining, bright, metal, artificial legs. I tried to scream but no sound came, the light gradually dimmed until it had all but disappeared, and then all I could see were the artificial legs moving steadily towards me. They had a life of their own, walking along the edge of the bed, until they were almost on top of me and I could see or sense nothing else — every joint, every screw — in absolute clarity of design and engineering skill.

Suddenly I shook myself awake, and realised I was upright, and that as I had been walking, I must have fallen asleep on my feet. My eyes tried to penetrate the gloom ahead, but there was no beam of light, no house. The tiredness in my legs had gone, they felt good and strong, and mine. My pace quickened.

Five

The ground felt hard to my head and I stirred restlessly until I awoke fully. I was in total darkness and I thought the harsh and uncomfortable ground had caused me to wake while it was still the middle of the night. I tried to close my mind and fall asleep again but consciousness refused to vanish and then I sat bolt upright as I realised I felt, or sensed light, on my face. I could not see. I rubbed my eyes trying to open them but the lids would not raise, there was some stickiness on them as if they had been coated with a glue. I stared intently ahead, trying to focus, trying to obtain some image, but to no avail. Panic rushed through me but I fought against the rising hysteria until I was finally able to calm myself somewhat and try to puzzle out what had happened. Perhaps I was still asleep and it was another dream or nightmare, but I felt very awake. Perhaps the sun had blinded me with its intensity; but when? I could feel no burning around my eyes or on my cheeks. Had some bird or insect dropped or laid something on my eyes which had made me temporarily blind? Because of the sticky feeling that seemed the most likely explanation to which I could cling. What I needed was water to bathe my eyes to try to clear them and clean away whatever was preventing my seeing. I reached out for my pack but could not locate it. I groped around on all fours trying not to move too far in any one direction, but still I could not find it. It would, I decided, be easier to work this out if I was upright so I stood up and stretching my arms forward to maintain balance, I took one step forward with my left foot and then pulled the right foot slowly towards it, at the same time prodding it left and right to see if it made any contact. I then took a step back to the original position and then another further back, repeating the process. I found nothing so I stepped forward to the original position and then towards the right side.

As I pressed down the ground fell away from beneath my foot and I toppled sideways and started to roll down an incline. It was a very steep slope and my hands tore at the bushes and brambles to try to stop myself from falling further but none of them had enough strength and they pulled out and came with me, if anything they seemed to aid my rapid descent. I soon reached the bottom of whatever it was I had descended and lay there bruised, winded and very afraid. I had no idea in which direction to go or what could be in front of me, only the all-consuming fear, would I ever regain my sight. I got into a sitting position and gingerly rubbed those places which had suffered particularly in my fall. After a while I realised it would do me no good sitting where I was, that I must try to go on and find someone or something that could help. I stood up feeling very sore, very bruised and very alone.

The sun was much hotter now and my throat was parched. The thought that I must find water acted as a spur to make me continue. I did not think I would gain anything by climbing back up the hill, and there was always the danger that I would slip and fall again. Should I go to the left or the right? In my state it did not matter, and I allowed my feet to lead me in any direction. I walked extremely slowly, feeling the ground ahead first with each foot, yet many times I stumbled and almost fell as I encountered some obstacle in my path. I listened intently to each noise to guide me, and I became more conscious of the sounds of birds and animals and even the flying insects that occasionally squeaked past my face. I heard a slight noise, more of a squeal really, to my right and turned towards it. It was gentle and soft and it continued as if the creature making it realised my predicament and weakness, and was itself totally unafraid. Slowly I walked towards the direction of the sounds which continued as if to guide me. When I thought I was practically on top of the creature making the sound, I stopped, bent down and imagined myself staring into the bright eyes of some field mouse, badger or other woodland creature. Cautiously I stretched out a hand trying to make contact, but immediately the squeaking ceased and there was nothing. I was alone again.

I continued walking, with slightly more confidence as I learned the trick of keeping the weight on my back foot while the advancing foot explored a safe resting point. I began to recognise the feel of the different textures of the soils and grasses and started to adapt to the contours of the ground. As I felt how uneven it was I realised it was full of movement and shape.

Suddenly a bird sang out, strongly, about head height, to my left; I felt pleased out of all proportion that I was able to make the simple deduction that there must be a tree close at hand. I felt my way towards it and my hand touched the rough bark, the shapes becoming meaningful as I explored the crevices, cracks and textures. Still the bird sang, totally unafraid of my presence, and I circled the tree two or three times to make a full exploration. I realised then that I had lost my previous sense of direction and now did not know which way to leave the tree to continue, as it was likely that I could be walking back the way I had come. I tried to recall the first touch of the tree in order to remember where I had started from but could not work it out. The bird called again and gave me the clue I needed. I kept the sound to my left as I stepped several paces to my right and the bird continued to sing as if to guide and encourage me. I stepped forward with more confidence. After a while the ground became steeper and I slowed my pace as I felt less sure of my steps. There was a breeze which helped to cool me and I felt slightly refreshed. Some specks of rain fell on my cheeks and I held my face upwards hoping the water would fall onto my eyes and face. But for a while nothing more seemed to fall and I went on slowly. Then, I felt more drops lightly touch my head. With a sudden and pleasing insight, I realised it was not rain I was feeling, but that the wind was blowing drops of water towards me. It meant that I must be very close to a river, lake or even an ocean, and, out of all proportion, I felt excited by this prospect, although I knew I now faced some kind of danger and must proceed with great caution. The ground was softer now, then muddy, and I bent down to touch it with my fingers. I heard the lapping of water and knew that sightless I was staring at whatever lay ahead. I crouched down, edging myself forward slowly to touch a bank with moss growing over it and knowingly my hands reached out to the water. I leaned forward, cupped my hands and rubbed the water on my eyes, threw it over my head and poured it into my mouth. I still could not see but at least I felt refreshed. When I had finished drinking, I edged back a few yards and lay down to rest. The lapping of the water was soothing and despite my desire not to sleep, I could not resist and I drifted into the inviting darkness of which I was already a part.

I awoke with a start and instantly remembered I would not see. Somehow I felt different; more afraid but less alone. That was it; I could feel someone or something standing over me. I could almost visualise a large shape blotting out the sun, staring into my sightless eyes. Perhaps it was a snake. I had a vision of a large cobra, poised to strike. My heart beat loudly, my body tensed, but I did not dare to speak. If I did and broke the silence, then whatever was there might attack. Perhaps it thought I was asleep — or even dead. But it could see my chest heaving furiously. Then it was gone and I was again alone. I called, "Wait. Please wait!" There was no reply. I crawled over to the water and drank again and splashed it over my head. I touched a log bumping along the shore and pushed it away, its texture was pliable and rubbery, and instantly, I realised what it was. I heard the loud snap of teeth and threw myself backwards, screaming, scrambling away on all fours, like some wounded beast. I kept going for as long as I could, climbing to higher ground all the time, until I could hear nothing and realised that nothing was in pursuit. Tears ran down my face; I knew now that water was barred to me and I would not dare to approach it again. I raised my arms, crying out in anger; angry with my weakness, my loneliness but most of all anger against anything that could see me but which could not be seen by me. Then as quickly as it had come, the anger subsided, only to be followed by a wave of self-pity which swept through me, causing my body to be racked with painful sobs until in my dejection and humiliation the tears flooded into my mouth and nose and I almost choked.

The grass sparkled green and fresh, and grew upwards in straight crisp lines. My tears continued to pour down, the drops bouncing away to catch at the tips of the grass and hang there like embryos of new life, before slowly trickling down to disappear into the earth beneath. As the realisation dawned on me, I fell forward almost swooning with the twin powers of the pain and the pleasure of knowing I could see again.

Six

I stood on the peak of a small hill and gazed down at a lake totally surrounded by forest. The trees were immense. Massive oaks, imposing tall pines and spread in amongst them huge, strange, twisted and tortured trees, totally leafless, yet with as much life as any of the others. They all seemed to lean away from me, but at the same time, in some odd way, they beckoned me forward, and over the intertwined branches I could see the dancing lights of the blue and green waters of the lake. They were like a thousand eyes staring out of focus. I strode briskly down and forward, my pace becoming slower as I reached them and started to push my way through the denseness of the outer trees. My progress was so slow that I thought I might have to retreat and try to find a way round them. The air had become thick and I was covered in perspiration; the cloying atmosphere causing an intense feeling of claustrophobia to overwhelm me as if its own life force depended on its taking over mine.

Just when I thought I could not go on any further and might have to fight my way back, a path suddenly and miraculously opened up before me and soon I was standing at the edge of the lake, its vast expanse peaceful, tranquil, offering friendship. The shore was littered with rotting tree trunks, soft and leathery to my touch. These were the crocodiles I had feared. I broke a piece of rotted wood which cracked in two sounding for all the world like teeth snapping at an unfortunate victim. I laughed freely, even crazily. I took off my shirt and sandals, and, after a moment's hesitation, the rest of my clothes and stood naked, part of the earth and the water. Time had no meaning. The water was not cold when I strode into it and I kept walking until it lapped over my chin and then I fell forward as if to sleep in the lake. I remained like that for a long time until slowly I lifted my arms to break the surface. I was facing away from the shore but felt I had drifted very far out. Something moved under my arm and then was gone so I would never know what it was. I felt very tired, perhaps the water was all I should ever need. I lay face down within its sweet embrace.

Something tugged at my legs, slowly wrapping around me. Looking down through the twisting movements of the lake I saw thousands of green tendrils of water vegetation moving agitatedly as if in protest at my intrusion into their kingdom. I tried to pull myself free but found that they were holding me fast and that as soon as I freed one leg, the other would become more entangled. I felt myself being sucked down below the surface of the water. For a few seconds only I panicked, but I was really too tired to struggle, somehow the majesty of the lake and its strength caused any fear to vanish and I felt myself in the presence of some force which was more important than life itself; certainly my life. I started to sink, knowing that I would not rise again. Then I saw the elephant. It was not a large elephant, not really like the sort of elephant that one sees in the Zoo, but probably that kind of elephant could not live under water. It did have a trunk though, which was why I thought it was an elephant, and this it curled round my body pulling me gently free from the vegetation and lifting me on to its back. It swam deeper into the lake using its ears as a means of moving through the water, then it started swimming further downwards with long powerful movements. I was neither swallowing water nor needing to breathe air, yet I felt no fear at such unusual events. The elephant reached a kind of plateau, swam to the top and came to rest. Gently it lifted me down from its back and placed me in front of it. I waited for it to do something else but the animal just looked patiently at me, and it too waited. Suddenly the water was moved violently and two grey shapes appeared, diving past me so closely as to almost push me to one side. They vanished for a few seconds and then reappeared.

Several times they repeated this sequence, each time getting slower yet each time becoming more violent in their actions. Then they were grey shapes no longer; they had fierce eyes, long snouts and rows of pointed teeth, they were, in fact, marauding sharks. I felt a fear which they seemed to sense, and they started their final dives towards me.

"Please help!" I shouted at the elephant, but it sat impassively, as if not seeing, certainly not seeming to care. I tried to run through the water but could not move with any speed. Only at the very last moment, by throwing myself to one side, was I able to avoid contact as the grey shapes hurtled past me. I was completely naked and had nothing with which to protect myself and I looked round for anything which I might use, but there was nothing.

"Why am I here?" I cried. The fear of the attack caused me to feel both the fear and the pain of death.

The sharks taunted me with their easy manoeuvres. I felt they were playing with me and could attack and kill whenever they chose, but I knew I had to keep trying to escape. The only place to hide was with the elephant. I rushed towards it and it appeared to look at me with an expression of understanding, and great sadness. I pulled at its trunk and crawled in between its legs as it sat impassively still. By leaning forward it could have crushed me, but I felt safer there than anywhere else. I could see the sharks circling as they decided how to get at me, for a moment I thought that they might be giving up and moving away. Then I saw their attack as they launched themselves at the elephant that was my protector. Their dark looming shadows blotted out all light and vision as they attacked in ferocious certainty. I felt the elephant stagger as they cut into its massive legs starting to tear away at them. Why did it not move? Why did it not protect itself? Why was it there? Why was I? The water was soon bloodied and the elephant must have been in terrible pain though I heard no cry. Still it stood protectively over me, its legs like ancient pillars. I could not allow the carnage to continue so I left my hiding place and started to run with slow movements towards what was, I vainly hoped, the direction of the shore. The way was clearer and indeed I seemed to be gaining speed, the currents of the water aiding me. Once I turned as I ran, and the waters cleared for a moment so that I saw what I took to be a smile on the elephant's face before it sank forward, its head resting on the ground as if in deep sleep.

I also saw the sharks — they were coming after me! They attacked in unison and tore at my arms, my shoulders, my legs. At first the pain was so intense I wanted to stop, then the pain was no more and only the running was important. Suddenly the water became shallower and I had reached the shore. I stumbled forward, falling several times, but each time managing to raise myself to keep moving forward. The water became too shallow for the sharks. I was alone. I fell to my knees and with the remaining vestiges of my strength crawled out of the water pulling myself further up the shore before rolling over on to my back to know no more.

The bright yellow sun beat down upon me. I awoke and remembered. I had been saved. I looked down at myself but there were no teeth marks, no wounds and no blood. Only memories.

Seven

It seemed a valley full of peace. Soft and lazy hillsides, lush grass, and the sun gently and quietly warming. It was empty, but for a horse, it was his valley. He trotted here and there, nibbling at small patches of grass, then cantering off until he found another patch to his liking. Tossing his head occasionally, his mane flowing out ruffled by a soft breeze, he would sometimes cock his head as if listening for something special. I heard nothing, perhaps there was nothing to hear, but the horse continued to listen. I decided to leave the horse to his kingdom. Although it would take me some hours longer to walk around the valley, I preferred to do so. The horse was aware of me, I was certain of that, but he obviously did not feel threatened, and carried on slowly sauntering over the grasslands. The sun was also moving around the valley, slowly looking for its resting place from the day. I saw one of the hills cast a long deep and wide shadow which reached almost to the horse, and the horse's shadow reached out to touch the larger shadow. The horse shied away moving some yards further on, its shadow now stretched out clear and untouched. The hill's long shadow reached out again to advance to merge with the smaller shadow of the horse. This was not possible! Shadows could not be cast from opposite directions, and the sun was behind the horse, not behind the hill. The massive shadow was much faster than any caused by a setting sun, and I realised it was not a shadow. It was some creeping and penetrating flood of black ink, spreading rapidly from the hill, always reaching out towards the shadow of the horse. I strained my eyes to see what was happening, and then realised that the edge of the shadow was not straight and clearly defined, but moved and shimmered slightly as if not sure of its own definition.

It was composed of thousands, perhaps millions, of black ants. The valley was being filled with them. They were trying to reach out towards the only living thing that was left in their path. The horse. Aware of them, he tried to ignore their invasion, possibly hoping they would go on through the valley, his valley, and leave him in peace once more. They had a different idea. They had eaten his shadow, and now they wanted the real thing. They swept past the horse, and for a moment, I thought that they might be going on through the valley, but they were merely making certain the horse could not escape them and were spreading themselves out, hemming the horse in to the side of the hill, and forcing him to withdraw to a small oasis. Now there was fear. The horse threw back his head and gave a long and fierce cry, perhaps that was the sound he had been listening for. Relentlessly the ants were eating the ground and space around the horse causing night to fall as they advanced. Soon the horse was left in a tiny semi-circle of sunlight that was continuously being eroded. The horse made one or two nervous runs towards the ants, as if to frighten them away, but they stood their ground, and it was his nerve that broke, each time he would stop just before he reached them, and back away to the slopes. He started to climb, the only way to go, but the ants kept coming forward and spread up the hill around him, at the same time starting to press in on both sides until he was forced to push himself harder and faster to try to escape. The slope was very steep and the horse found it difficult to keep his footing, slipping and sliding down and then in panic he would force himself up a few yards further as the ants advanced. The horse was sweating, white saliva coming out of his mouth, his head thrashing from side to side as he strained to maintain his ascent.

No longer was the sun a gentle friend, it beat down fiercely. The horse's coat glistened with sweat, and it was caked with dust as the hill became more and more hostile. It thrust him backwards as if in sacrifice to the ants. The horse's legs began to buckle, and he was slowing. He was in a nightmare of no return. The ants were the night, and soon night would have taken over, and the day of the horse would have gone. Exhausted, his legs unable to move forward, the horse slipped and fell, got up unsteadily, stumbled forward, then fell to his knees, in final surrender. He turned his head and looked directly at me. No longer proud, he was pleading for help, but I turned away and took the longer walk around the valley. I did not hear any screams.

Eight

I discovered the glass quite accidentally. The day had been overcast, sticky and oppressive. There were thick swatches of cloud covering the sky, a storm felt imminent. The sun had tried valiantly to break through on a few occasions, but each time had been thwarted, banished back to his kingdom by two powerful clouds that rushed together to lock arms against his approach. However, he kept trying to achieve a breakthrough, always in vain, until at last he saw a chance, and through a narrow gap in the clouds, that they neglected immediately to guard, a single ray of sunlight shone triumphantly through, like a golden rod casting a spell on the spot where it struck. The ground sparkled in response, and then I saw the glass. It reflected smaller golden rods of magic which, for a brief moment, drew to it in wonderment the insects and birds that were hurrying by to escape the expected storm. The clouds roared in fury at this impertinence and crashed together to cast out this intrusion. Once more the earth was in darkness, but too late, I had seen the glass. At first I could not be certain that it would not be just a polished stone that had attracted my attention, and I hurried towards the spot where I had seen its radiance to investigate. It was not lying on top of the ground, it was half buried, part of its milky white top jutting out. I tried to loosen it, but it was larger than it first appeared and I had to dig away quite a lot of earth from around it in order to prise it free. It seemed to be entirely glass. It was oval in shape, domed, and with a flat bottom. Gently I cleaned away the rest of the mould and earth and placed it on a rock to examine it more carefully. It had several colours in it, those visible at any moment depending upon the angle from which it was observed. Sometimes it was predominantly blue, or green, or white. Cool to the touch, when

I stroked it, my hand recoiled as I felt it vibrate. I replaced my hand, but felt no further vibration, possibly I had imagined it.

I heard a high pitched whine; at first I did not realise it was coming from the glass itself, then the sound increased. There seemed to be movement from within. Although the surface remained still it was full of coloured liquids continually flowing and creating vibrant colourful movements. There were shapes and shadows formed within it which at first did not resemble anything, but gradually took on more solid shape and became the figures of men, four men fighting a fifth. The fifth had only a sword whilst the others each had a shield, and a spear, as well as a sword. They confidently moved forward, and the lone defender was hard pressed under threat of conquest. The miniature figures were quite real and I could see the fear in the eyes of the man about to be killed. I wanted to intervene to prevent his death. Finally his sword was knocked from his hand and he fell to the ground; the others laughed, pausing for a moment before raising their swords and spears, ready to plunge them in him. Without waiting, not even considering the outcome, I picked up a nearby stone and smashed it at the glass which instantly shattered into many pieces, the colours and the liquids flowing out and away. I tried to find the men, but there were only stains on the ground and whatever I had seen in the glass was lost. I picked up a piece of the broken glass to examine it and saw that it had been hollow with a double outer rim. The glass was jagged and I cut a finger deeply, my blood started to pour out and fall in huge drops to the ground. I thought it was just a minor cut and the flow would quickly stop, but it did not, and I became dizzy from the loss of blood and within moments found myself collapsing to the ground. Everything swam within my head, I felt very dazed and light headed. Gradually I recovered and stood up, still somewhat shaky, and realised that I must have fallen into deep thick grass and I had to push quite hard to make my way through it.

I saw a giant black bird flying overhead, one much larger

than I had ever seen before, it looked quite evil and very ferocious, as it turned towards me it seemed too interested for comfort, I ran for cover hiding myself in between some nearby boulders. The bird which was even more gigantic close to, tried to reach me among the boulders but could not get its beak through and eventually gave up, flying away in disgust. Quite shaken I left my sanctuary. Looking around I could see a large glass wall, the height of a house, strangely shaped and with very sharp edges. In growing bewilderment, I came to realise that it resembled exactly part of the glass object I had broken. At first I tried to dismiss the thought, but it would not go away, and eventually I had to face the fact that I had somehow become miniaturised and the giant grass in which I was standing was the ordinary grass that had previously been beneath my feet, and the bird that had seemed so immense and evil was merely an ordinary blackbird.

Everything had become a major obstacle and I had to scramble around boulders and rocks many times my size, which before would have been simply pebbles or tiny stones. I heard and felt many rustlings in the grass around me, and I had obviously become the object of curiosity to all kinds of insect creatures which previously had been of no consequence to me. I tried to avoid them and keep my distance, but there were so many. I almost fell across a very large speckled beetle that eyed me with great interest and then started to advance towards me with a speed that I could not match. I ran as hard as I could, but unused to the terrain, in my panic I fell over, and the beetle reached me, took a firm grip of me and started to squeeze. I felt myself blacking out in pain and felt it would shortly be the end, when a bloodied figure rushed forward towards me. It was the swordsman that I had tried to save and now with a blow from his sword he stabbed and killed the beetle and I was free. I gasped my thanks as he threw down his sword to help me up, I embraced him with gratitude. Then to my horror, not being able to utter a warning, I saw the other four swordsmen approach him from behind and before I could release my arms they had driven their swords through his body and I felt the sword points enter mine also, and impaled we fell together.

I shook my head and opened my eyes. The finger had stopped bleeding. Some yards away a blackbird peered closely at the ground, seized a black beetle in its beak and then flew off with it.

Night

I walked faster. I had lost too much time in thinking, wild and crazy thoughts. A wide-eyed, hungry raven had screeched past me its cry helping to keep me in motion. For a time I even ran. The distant hills loomed blue and misty, beckoning me on. A bank of yellow sunflowers over to my right kept crowding into my eye line so that the blues and yellows mixed to give an iridescent green haze to the foliage that covered the valley floor. There was no apparent path yet somehow I was following one. Possibly there had been one a thousand years ago, and its invisible lines were guiding me with echoes of feet that had gone before. My steps led me downwards and as the light started to fade the shadow of a devil bat swooped past, fleeing from or in pursuit of something unknown. Further down away to the left I could see a very large stone with another much smaller one positioned on top and their shapes drew me towards them.

As I neared the boulders the size of the main one increased until I could no longer see the one on top, the lower one overshadowing everything and preventing any further sighting of the smaller one. It was becoming very dark now with only the vaguest shimmerings of light occasionally bouncing off the mountains. I decided to sleep the night at its base, and half asleep already, dropped my pack down in front of it.

I do not know what suddenly decided me to explore around the large boulder before going to sleep. It was extremely hard, probably some kind of granite, and yet was surprisingly smooth, and free of any indentation or crack. A fierce flash of dying sun arrowed through a mountain opening and for a moment the boulder gleamed and glittered with a shimmering yellowish glow. I counted my paces and reached my pack on twenty-one. The height of the lower boulder alone must have been over fifteen feet but because of its curvature I could not see the top and with my curiosity aroused I decided to climb up before the light went totally. The thought was much easier than the deed, as there were no holds or anything jutting out on which to pull myself up over the rim of the boulder. I piled together some small rocks and stones and parts of a dead tree and by stacking them precariously together was just able to set up some steps on which I could climb. It was a bit of a scramble but somehow I was able to slide myself forward, arms outstretched and wriggle on to the top. The small boulder was a much smaller stone and perfectly rounded. It was so smooth and so evenly circular that it was some moments before I realised it was rotating extremely slowly. I was tired of course, very tired, perhaps to the point of exhaustion, but it was definitely rotating. My first instinct was to retreat but I overcame that and edged forward on my haunches to look more closely. It was now so very dark that the absence of light played strange tricks, and the stone almost seemed to be swaying, moving backwards and forwards, first towards me then away. Then in a very slow drawn-out movement which took minutes to accomplish the stone divided into two and a piercing light from it revealed a small mirror which appeared to hang in its centre without any visible support. Oval in shape, the mirror was unframed, and at first all I could see in it was my own face staring wide-eyed back at me with no reflection of anything behind me. My reflection then vanished and I could look through the mirror as if it was a magnifying glass and clearly see the valley beyond. The glass focused on a multi-coloured butterfly asleep on a mottled dark brown leaf and I could see them both in absolute detail and with complete clarity. Briefly my own image reappeared and I reached out to touch it but did not make contact.

"Why me", I thought, " and why now?" I felt the mirror's reply. "You are here and here am I; others have come but have not seen what they want and maybe you will not. I can show you what you see and what you would like to see but you may want your own truth which is not my truth, and then you will break me, but I will always be here." There was so much to know. How could I ask my questions and hear the truth? The mirror darkened and then once more became clear, and again I saw the butterfly. "Is it asleep?" "No," the reply came. "It is dead, because you saw it as dead and that is the truth." I looked again and there was no butterfly. I tried hard to think of living and beautiful things, but all I could see were thick black clouds rolling through the valley until they merged with the smoke emitted from guns and I heard the cries of dying men and the screams of horses. I saw a small group of horsemen surrounded by hundreds of attackers who would not give up until they had destroyed them. Theirs was a bloody and barbarous death. "Why did I see these things?" I asked aloud. First a butterfly, then the horsemen. The valley became a holocaust of terror until nothing was left but empty barren terrain; lifeless and disfigured, black and desolate; except that is, for a butterfly that fluttered its wings and started to fly directly towards me. The mirror moved and glinted and in it reflected I saw an attacking bird diving with screeching open beak towards the butterfly which slowed as if to offer itself up as an easy sacrifice. I shouted a warning but it went unheeded and I threw myself at the mirror, trying to reach the valley putting myself between the butterfly and the raven's beak. Somehow I managed it, I knew not how; and felt a terrible pain as the beak tore into me instead. Under the bird's anger of frustrated desire, in great pain I fell backwards and downwards, but with the vision of a fragile butterfly fluttering away to safety.

When I awoke the pain had gone, the early sun was striking my face and I was still lying at the foot of the larger boulder. I drank some water before setting off again down the valley.

Ten

At first it had looked like some massive natural grouping of rocks and stones that had been thrown up by forces of past milleniums, suddenly and inexplicably found in remote deserts or starkly marking out a wide and otherwise monotonous plateau. I was naturally drawn towards it and it was only when I got quite close that I realised it was man-made. It was an ancient temple of magnificent proportions. Everything a temple should be. Huge stone pillars, ornately carved at the top and bottom stretching skywards, in the middle round and smooth as a woman's skin, they supported part of a curved stone roof of immense size. The pillars themselves had been raised with flights of steps, well over fifty, leading up to the base of each corner pillar.

What was all this doing here in the middle of this wilderness, a valley totally inhospitable and barren, its soil seemingly not able to support even the lowest vegetation, the ground cracked and dry as if from countless years of drought?

Then I realised the temple was inhabited. What were all those people doing? For this was no abandoned relic of a bygone age, there were hundreds of men and women milling around it. The men were mostly turbaned, though some had shaven heads, and the women wore long flowing, colourful robes that covered and obscured their bodies except when climbing the steps their garments would swing open to reveal their naked legs, which hinted at a promise of further nakedness above. They walked as if they knew where they were going, but they were going nowhere. They walked up the steps and into the temple, and then walked out of the temple and down the steps and around the stone sides to begin again. They would not leave the sanctuary of the stones themselves nor put a foot on the ground beyond the temple and the steps. Inside, the temple was divided into a series of small chambers each with roof or ceiling, and sometimes groups of several men, or women, would enter one, stand there for a few minutes, and then leave and return to being solitary walkers continuing as before. As they all looked alike, it was difficult to follow one individual person as he or she vanished into a crowd of similarly garbed people. However, by concentrating on one person at a time, sometimes I was able to maintain contact, and follow the strange ritual through. I saw that he or she would eventually end up in the same spot as before, and after a few moments the whole process would start again. I decided to approach the temple, and to mingle with them. They kept their heads averted, and did not react to my presence. They felt like real people, and I deliberately bumped into some of them in order to touch or when I stood in their way they accidentally brushed past me, but they never spoke to me or to one another. In fact there was a total absence of sound in the whole process. When I realised this, I tried to listen for the fall of their footsteps, but there was none, possibly because they were all barefoot and the stones did not give off any sound or vibration. Even the air was still. The whole movement was continuous, the people resembled a colony of ants full of determined activity, but there was no real purpose and no end result.

I do not know when the rumblings started, but one moment there was the continuing silence, the next a number of vibrations which increased in sound and velocity, so that the ground itself began to shake, and caused the temple pillars to shudder. It felt like the beginnings of an earthquake, and I tried to run out and down the steps so that I would be away from the pillars if they were to crash down. It was as if the crowd tried to impede my progress, and there now seemed to be more of them than before, but they were not paying any attention to the loud insistent sounds that I could hear. I pushed and fought my way to about half way down the stairs when the first crash occurred. One of the pillars tore itself free of its foundation and part of the roof crashed just ahead of me. Everyone in its path was crushed, and I narrowly escaped being hit. With one support gone, the rest of the roof reacted even more violently to the next earth cry, crashing down in all directions throwing huge blocks of stone masonry which pinned people down, slowly crushing and mangling their bodies. At least now they were emitting sound, I could hear their screams and cries of agony. I could not imagine how I had not been hit, and then I looked up and saw a huge block of stone falling directly towards me. Fear petrified me also into stone. There was no way I could escape and for a long, slow moment I waited for the impact, and everything else seemed to slow down and come to a stop around me as if everyone was watching and waiting for me to be crushed. As in slow motion I raised my hands above my head in what seemed a vain attempt to protect it. Yet as they touched the stone I felt it float away as if made of cardboard, and it crashed a few yards further on immediately pinning down and killing at least four or five others. I was shocked at my escape and could not understand it. All around me were the signs of death and destruction. Then another pillar was torn from its base and came hurtling towards me at an incredible speed. Again I stretched out both hands and as I made contact the stone pillar swung itself around, missing me and rolling down the steps crushing everyone in its path. It seemed I alone had a charmed life and could not be killed.

I could not understand and in a state of bewilderment wandered back into the centre of the temple and stood there whilst it continued to crash around me. Each time anything came near me I was able either to deflect it and watch it spin away or else miraculously it would miss me and I was able to stand there, shocked, but unhurt. Eventually nothing was left standing, not even one stone on top of another and even the stone steps had cracked into a thousand fissures, with gaping holes into which the bodies tumbled. No one else was alive, everything had been destroyed. The vibrations, the violence,

47

the earthquake stopped, and the air became clear and clean again. It was as if the earthquake had never occurred, certainly not for centuries, only the ruins told the story.

I left the ruined temple and continued on my way. The rest of the valley was as sparsely covered and incapable of supporting any worthwhile life as much as the land around the temple had been. I started a long climb and did not stop until I had put a great deal of distance between myself and the destruction. After a while I found some water, a mountain spring, and was able to refresh myself. I climbed a little higher and then looked back down the valley. The light was going but I could still see. The temple was standing erect, magnificent and strong as if it had stood there for a thousand years, perhaps five thousand, and from this high point I could again marvel at it and wonder how it had been created. The distance was very great and it was difficult to make out any real detail from where I stood but the steps of the temple seemed to be black with ants that scurried into it and then out again.

Dragonfly

I never knew her age. When I first saw her I thought she was fifteen or sixteen, then as I got to know her and saw her at different times, asleep, or just stretching herself awake in the early hours of the morning, she seemed so frail and innocent that I would have accepted eleven or twelve, although there were times when her face turned in upon itself and her wide staring eyes became sunken and full of fear, then her age doubled and trebled, even her way of walking aged so that she stooped and shuffled like a woman of the fields. Her age does not matter, I knew her for a lifetime, although she had lived a lifetime before I met her. Sometimes I wondered how old she thought I was. That didn't matter either, because I knew she had come to love me, her trust in me was more important to her than time and life, and my bringing life to her had given mine back to me. That was a very long time ago, but still there is not a day without my thinking of her, and more and more often I become so confused as I think I am she, or she is me, and when I see people looking at me oddly I always think that it is because they are seeing her face; it is suddenly like hearing a dumb person speak or talking to people before you know they cannot hear.

There were a lot of people along the route; most of them had given up, some rejected, all abandoned. Some had signs around their necks. One read 'derelict', another 'condemned', yet another 'dangerous', a fourth 'unsafe'. Some signs were blank so whatever words of destruction were best suited to that particular shell of a person could be filled in. Hidden or invisible, the signs were there, and I could see them clearly. As I passed, I looked closely at each one, but no one looked back at me, and our eyes never met. I was just a passing ghost, and they knew they could not and should not touch me, and that if they had tried their hands would pass right through me. They knew they were rejects, their assembly line had long ceased to operate, and they were rusting into oblivion. If only their oblivion would come before the rats of madness were able to chew completely through.

After a while I too ceased to see them, their shapes becoming more indistinct. As soon as I could I turned off this avenue of pain and left them all far behind. But as soon as I could not see them the shapes formed again, and became distinct and their gaunt lined faces and painfully swollen bellies were edged in sharp black lines so clearly defined I could really touch them. It took me many miles and many more hours before I was able to wipe those lines away, and cease to hear silent and reproachful cries ebbing and flowing, aimlessly washed backwards and forwards.

The dark thoughts banished themselves, my head ceased throbbing and I could enjoy the sweetness and peacefulness again. It was such a beautiful day. The shafts of warm sunlight guided my feet down the pathways, and the air was fragrant and seductive. Then the memories crowded back. Had they really been there? Who were they, and where had they come from? There was certainly nowhere for them to go. Was their futility, their hopelessness meant to show me a contrast to the beauty of the world I inhabited? The fragility of a dragonfly brushed past me, and as its name implies, it had power, force, and determination, a strength a thousand times greater than any of the dismal creatures that I had left squatting in the distance so far behind. With a suddenness I could not control I snatched at the dragonfly and caught it, crushing it in my hands, but it did not die instantly. It fluttered its broken wings, as if to say — what has this accomplished, you have not saved one of them — and then it died. I know it was right, I had crushed it because I could not save them. The dragonfly was unafraid to die for it knew it had lived, even though they had not.

The shame of my acts, now and before, choked me, somehow I found the courage to turn around, to turn back, to try to find them. I wished the dragonfly could know, but it could not and all I could do now was to offer myself.

The road changed, it laughed at me as it sent me first this way and then another way, down paths I had not trod, along tracks which were utterly alien. There had been my moment of truth when I could have stopped and sat amongst them, by joining them could have helped, perhaps only one of them, made just one my friend, but now none would ever know that I had even tried.

She was sitting on a small tree stump, head lowered, eyes on the ground, feet turned protectively inwards. I could not see much of her face but could sense the beauty in her. She was very thin, and wore an even thinner dress. I made a noise with my feet to try to attract her attention but she did not look up. I took off my shadow and let it fall over her putting her into darkness but she did not react, as she was already in darkness. I felt I could not approach her without her first encouraging me to do so, so I slowly walked by, half turned towards her so that I could respond immediately to her slightest gesture or sound. There was none, and I had to continue walking. I covered fifty yards, and still she had not made one movement. She was not waiting, yet she waited. When about to die, one place is very much like another. I did not want her to die, but I could not save her, nor did I know how I could. Did she want me to save her? To stand between someone and death, and then to stand back is to allow a double death. If I could not deal with my own life, and the responsibility of it, how could I take on her responsibility. I stopped and sat down watching her until the sun started its final descent and the shadows lengthened, creating a mirror world where substance became merely an intruder. Her shadow did not lengthen and it stayed thin. She had become thinner during the time I watched her.

Then I saw the snake, dark green, and fat. It looked as

if it had already eaten very well that day but just the same it decided to eat again. It edged towards the girl in short vibrating movements. It was perhaps fifty yards from the girl before the full realisation of its intentions hit me and then I knew I must intervene and take on the responsibility for my intervention. A small mottled frog stood transfixed with fear in the path of the snake, but the snake brushed it aside as if of no account. It was after bigger prey. The frog rolled over, certainly incapable of movement or escape, and if it was not yet dead from fright, the snake would settle its fate when it returned.

I was shouting, running and shouting, waving, yelling. The girl paid no attention, did not hear, did not see, and did not respond. Surely she must sense the snake which seemed to grow larger with every yard that it closed in upon her. My heart was pounding, my brain was racing. It had become the most important thing in the world for me to reach her in time and kill the snake, or at least put myself between it and the girl. I knew I was going to arrive too late. I stopped, found a stone and in what I felt was a futile gesture I threw it at the snake. The stone seemed to float slowly in the air, spinning and twisting and as I willed it on, the snake raised itself ready to strike. The stone suddenly hurtled forward and struck the snake directly in its fangs; stunned and shocked at this outrage the snake reared backwards, turned and vanished into the shadows. Still the girl had not moved, her head and eyes had remained facing downwards and she had not responded, neither to the attack of the snake nor to my own intervention. I was shut out, but this time I would not leave. I would break down the doors, I leaned forward and cupped her face in my hands. She looked up and saw me, she rose and I picked her up and cradled her and I felt her cling to me, she had accepted me and I was a man again.

I fed her, washed her, giving her the strength I had and in doing so gained even more. She would go with me wherever I took her. She never spoke, but her eyes had and that was enough. I never needed a name to call her, she was always there, but to myself I called her Dragonfly. She would always have fragile wings but would need the courage and determination a dragonfly has.

Twelve

It took many days before I was able to gain her confidence fully. From the beginning she trusted me, but was always full of fears, and would shy away like a frightened colt. Any unexpected sound or noise would make her jump, fear was always just below the surface, ready to be awakened at any moment. Unable to speak and talk out her fears, the terror that she felt became magnified in her face which had to express everything she felt. In seconds her face could change from being relaxed, almost placid, to a wide-eyed expression shattered with abject terror.

Gradually, I gained ascendency over her fears, and she began to rely on me and bestow upon me her absolute trust. I made certain I was always there when she was awake, and I tried never to go to sleep until she had. It always seemed strange the way I could hear her breathing, but had never heard her speak or utter another sound. As she slowly gained in confidence I hoped that suddenly she would speak, and I would hear her voice, even if I could not understand what she was saying; but she never did. Although we learned to communicate, and I talked freely to her, and I think she understood, she never responded with one word, a sound, not even a scream or cry. At first she was afraid to show me her body, and I thought she must have been beaten or tortured. I always turned away and left her completely alone whenever she bathed or washed. However, as her confidence increased, she was able to undress in front of me and jump unconcernedly into the water, and I was grateful for her trust. In fact there were no marks on her body; only her mind, having seen so much, had suffered the marks. She was part of the suffering of the others, having experienced the terrors they had gone through. She was a light sleeper, and often I would wake up and find her sitting, motionless, expressionless, staring into the distance, watching for something that she hoped she would never see again. When she realised I was awake she would quickly smile, lie down again and go to sleep. When she did not see I was awake, I would watch her quietly and wonder at the thoughts that lay hidden behind her face. Always I would remain awake waiting for her to lie down again, and for her slow breathing to commence, then I could also relax and sleep. Over a period of time the visions that she had within started to fade and she was obviously learning to like the world again. But most of all I knew she liked Exit, and I became her world. For brief moments I felt the responsibility of her was too much to handle and I almost wished that I was on my own again. Those moments passed quickly and the delights and joy she brought me overcame all my reservations, helping me to blot out the blackened memories that would crowd into my mind since the aeroplane had crashed. She knew nothing of this or my background, and what had started me on this journey, although I knew she felt that I had my own sorrow. She was just happy to be with me and to try and give me the same comfort and relief I offered her. We were an odd pair, and yet we needed one another. She was perhaps a third of my age, yet my equal in misery. We both needed something, and I hoped that we would find what we needed at the same time. Maybe it was the same thing.

Tragic Thirteen

Dragonfly wanted to run on ahead and I was happy to let her. She was really excited and high spirited and her glow seemed to light up everything as she passed it by. The rocks shimmered and their edges were sharp like razors. She danced on and on, and I would almost have sworn there were moments when her feet were gliding over the ground like a petite human hovercraft. She would disappear around a curve in the hillside, and when I finally came to it and rounded it she was nowhere to be seen; then her silent laugh would touch me and I would turn round and she would be behind me excitedly jumping from one foot to the other, her toes shooting out little specks of dust. I never could find out how she did it, but it happened time and time again, until I gave up wondering and just enjoyed the fun until my smile equalled hers and our smiles would link hands and we would proceed together.

She was running on as before and again disappeared from sight. I came up to where she should have been but she was not there. I waited, but could feel nothing, turned around, and she was still not there. I walked on a few yards, and spun round, but Dragonfly was nowhere in sight. I felt uneasy but not really panicky, and thought she must be playing a new kind of game and I would quickly find out what it was about. But she did not come back. Not that day. Nor any time through the night. I did not sleep. Then it was morning again. I did not know where to go. I was frightened of leaving the place where she had vanished, in case she made her way back there. I wanted to rush ahead in case she had gone much further on than I had thought, and had either got lost or had fallen and hurt herself, but I did not dare to do that. I decided to place my pack on a high and visible point and then I kept circling around from it looking behind rocks, in crevices, in any hole I could find, but always keeping my position to the pack and working my way back to it so that I myself did not get lost.

I had no smiles left, and no tears either. Sometimes I thought I had even stopped breathing, but it was only my turning off another sense perhaps to prevent my giving way to another emotional outburst, and after a while I would hear again my laboured breathing as my faltering steps drove me round and round in increasing circles of deeper despondency. I felt dulled, like a blunted knife that could not cut through the gloom she had left behind, I felt unclear and confused. Just before it became dark again, I saw something glittering on the ground, it was a gold coin. I picked it up and saw there was another one next to it, and then more. I had started to pick them up before the realisation struck me, and then shaking with horror I threw them far away. I knew someone was paying me for Dragonfly. Someone thought I would be willing to sell her; but that was not true, and she could never be bought from me, even if she could be taken.

Again there was total darkness, and in my concern I had lost sight of where I had placed my pack. I did not dare move in case I wandered in the wrong direction, and I sat cross-legged on the ground to wait for morning to arrive. I had some matches and occasionally I tried to light one so that she could see where I was in case she was looking for me, but each time the wind blew the flame out. A number of times I burnt my fingers, but did not feel any pain, yet I knew the pain would come in the morning. Weariness caused my head to nod, and I would throw it back forcing myself awake in case I was wanted. A cry would ring out, but it would not be her cry. The grey morning light crept in and touched my haggard face with its greyness. It attached itself to my face and there was no way to shake it off and my eyes also were covered with a grey mist.

I started to shout her name and then to shout anything that came into my head. It was only the sound she might hear, but she could not hear the words. The words hovered around me, uncertain where to go, and then would change into darting little sparrows and would swoop away to join a passing flock and leave, never to return. The words did not look back and I knew they were gone forever. Occasionally I would wet the words with tears trying to weight them down so they would escape less easily, but as soon as they had gone a short way they would shake themselves so that the tears ran down and away, and each word would then sweep freely upwards, unrestrained and out of my control, provided it did not look back, and it did not want to look back, it wanted to escape. Perhaps Dragonfly had been happy to escape, but I buried that dagger where it belonged in the deepest hole, and blocked it up with a huge stone and put even more stones on top of it so that it could never surface.

Fourteen

I had been totally alone for days. Dragonfly had not come back and I could not find her, but I would carry her with me always, and I would not let her down. Perhaps I would find another Dragonfly, but even as I thought it I knew that could not be. I was truly on my own again. I had not come across even the smallest wild creature. Even the odd bird had been so far away that I could not hear its cries and it had floated through the air like a dying leaf. The way was hard and rocky and very unfriendly. I climbed higher along the mountain path, having to stop more often to catch my breath as the effort and lack of oxygen began to take its toll. There was a stillness and a silence which weighed heavily upon me, it was not easy to keep on, although there was no alternative. Suddenly the road started to ease downwards, and descending was much easier and my spirits lifted as my pace quickened. Now there were little mountain flowers along the path, bright and welcoming, the wind moving them gently so that they beckoned me with enquiring eyes. They seemed to be almost talking, I could hear a gentle whisper which grew and grew as I walked further along into a hubbub of sound, and strange voices. I half ran the last few yards to the bend in the path and as I turned it, there set out below was a town, not large, but with very tall buildings crowded together and overshadowed streets full of people, animals and shops of all kinds. I looked down at them but they did not look up at me. They were too busy for that. The people seemed from their faces and clothes to be oriental. Most had pigtails and they wore long flowing multi-coloured robes and each person had the same black-eyed exotic expression. Something hung from out of almost every window, washing, drying fruit or even children and women, all shouting and gesticulating to others across from or below them.

The path led quickly down and I soon reached the main street which was even more crowded at that level than it had seemed from above. I was taller than they were, dirty, ragged and white skinned even though burned from many days in the sun. Yet no one seemed to see me, no one stopped to look and no one approached. I felt conspicuous yet at the same time ignored. At a stall, colourfully decorated and full of lemons, oranges and other fruits which I did not recognise, I hesitatingly asked in English, "How much?" Although the stall owner gave no indication he had not understood my question he did not respond in any way and my question was ignored — and I was ignored.

"How much?" "How much?" "How much?" Each time I repeated the question I edged nearer until I stood opposite the stallholder staring into his closed face. The eyes did not answer, nor did his voice, but he reached down and picked up two oranges and held them out. I took them and he moved away without asking for any payment. I peeled the oranges. The fruit was sweet and juicy and the juice trickled down my chin. I let the peel drop to the floor and an old woman, shapeless in a shapeless black dress, shuffled forward and picked it up and carried it away. I was shamed by her simple action and looked to see who else had noticed but no one seemed to be watching me or paying any attention. I walked down the street and joined other groups at various stalls and in shops trying to see what reaction there would be but each time I was ignored as if I were invisible or unclean. Sometimes I would force my attention upon someone who would eventually respond but without involvement, always giving me whatever I demanded, yet never asking for payment, and always moving away immediately afterwards. I could not make any contact with anyone. I tried to approach a cat that sprawled across a doorway half in and half out of the shafts of sunlight, but as I bent down to stroke it a throaty roar was emitted and the cat rolled to its feet and disappeared inside the shop. I walked further into the town, the streets becoming narrower, the buildings crowding upon each other even further so that little sunlight could penetrate, only the reflections from the buildings and the windows created any light with which to see. It became even more dusty and the people here were busier and still seemingly unaware of my presence.

Most of the buildings were decayed and broken, and there were great ruts in the streets which had become filled with black mud that had baked in the stifling atmosphere. A man selling fish had laid out the dead fish in even rows according to size and kind. The one eye that stared upwards was the only thing that seemed to focus upon me and I wondered if it would have looked at me had the fish been alive. There was a very strong smell so I hurried away down one of the side streets. As I neared a doorway a woman suddenly stepped out and turning away walked along the street in front of me. I slowed so as not to bump into her, then I realised that she did not walk in the same shuffling way as the others, that she was better dressed and that her movements were more deliberate, even suggestive. I stopped to consider this and after a few yards she too stopped, turned, and faced me. She was strikingly beautiful with bright eyes and shining lips. She looked straight at me. She, like the others, was oriental in appearance, but she was giving me a wide smile and this contrast to the others' response stunned me. She swayed slightly as if to show herself off, then slowly her lips kissed the air provocatively. Half turning and still looking at me, she entered a building to my right. I deliberated whether or not to follow, then I became aware that for the first time there were others in the street looking at me. They were not smiling and I could feel their anxious looks upon my back as I decided to follow her.

There was a small, dark hallway and then a flight of stairs. I could hear her footsteps mounting higher as I started to climb after her. The building was taller than I had expected and I kept climbing flights of stairs which twisted and turned before I reached a door at the very top. The door would not open. It was locked. Then I saw the key in the lock, turned it and the door opened. It was a very white room with a large, open, full-length window, a stand with a bowl of water, a chair and a bed. There was no one in the room. Crossing to the window, I looked across the tiny alley way to the house beyond.

There, was a similar room and in it was the woman, still with her provocative smile. I looked at the room below that one, and there she was again, again smiling and inviting. I looked into every room and she was in each one. I felt shaken and drained as I realised that I had followed an illusion. I turned to retrace my steps only to find that the door was again shut and locked. I remembered the key on the outside. I seemed to know what was expected of me, moved to the window and stepped out. I floated for a moment before my speed accelerated and I hit the ground with a thud which caused clouds of dust to swirl into the air to cover and hide me, and everything else, so I could neither see nor be seen.

I was by the roadside and my face was wet from the black rain that had fallen in the early morning. I sat up quickly but knew in advance I would see no town, no street, no beautiful oriental woman, just the road ahead. My head throbbed, and as the pain increased, I sank back onto the road and gradually lost consciousness again.

Fifteen

Although not perfect the light had been quite sufficient for walking, then in only a few seconds the change to complete darkness had occurred. Although I could not see the way ahead I obviously could not stop where I was. My pace slowed to a hesitant stumble and I struck my feet time and time again on stones and other obstacles in my path. I'm certain they could have been heard before the light had faded so abruptly, but I had not been aware of them, now the night was full of sound and soft rustlings, sudden movements and the cries of flying or crawling creatures. The noises they made seemed to increase with every hesitant step I took. The ground gave way to soft sinking moss into which my feet started to sink, it became a laboured effort to continue. I felt as if I was sinking further and further and did not dare risk going on for fear of falling into a swamp or marsh which would make me only too welcome. The clouds parted for a moment, a brief shaft of moonlight shone spotlighting a fiercesome object that suddenly reared up on my left side. Its arms stretched outwards, but it was only the interplay of light and shade that gave it a false malevolence. It was only a tree. I clutched it with great relief feeling comfortable and relaxed from just being there and being allowed to use it for support. I decided to pull myself up into its branches until morning, but could not find a lower branch with which to start, and after circling the tree once I did not really feel I could attempt to climb up in safety. I lowered my pack to the ground and took out my last apple. The sound of my eating echoed through the night and all the other creatures stilled as if listening in bewilderment to this alien noise. I finished the apple and threw the core into the distance but did not hear it land. In the blackness it was as if it had vanished immediately upon leaving my hand. I reached back for the tree and almost over balanced as my hand came into contact with empty air. I spun round in every direction, stabbing with both hands at the darkness, but could not make contact with anything. Had I wandered away without realising it? My foot prodded my pack and I knew I remained in the same position. It was the tree that had moved. I tried to recall what it had really been like. Could it have been an animal or some other creature? I tried to re-create all the remembered images thrown up by that one sighting and my touch. I just knew it had been a tree, but then how could it vanish? Was there a hole in the ground where its roots had been embedded? I bent down and groped in the darkness. My hands felt the softness of the mossy earth but could not locate any depression or gap into which a tree might have been rooted. I was bewildered by this strange and inexplicable happening. I could not help but throw my arms upwards in dramatic expression, the fingers outstretched. For a brief moment the clouds again parted and the moonlight shone directly down and I could see myself. I was the tree! I tried to move my arms and touch myself, but they were immobile. I could not turn my head, nor look down, nor could I move or use my legs. Without having to actually see them, I became aware of the trees that were positioned around, some sombre and majestic, leafy, with multitudes of branches, others more like myself, just a trunk and two or three branches, jutting out as if in supplication to the sky. More moonlight shone through the blackness and I realised trees were like humans, needing light to see and sleeping when there was no light. I heard an owl in a nearby tree and wondered if it would come to me. I wanted to be a tree that birds liked and used and not one alone and unvisited. A small creature, possibly a mouse, ran around my feet, the base of the tree, and then was gone but the contact was exciting. I wanted something else to touch me and I waited hopefully, but nothing came. Everything was now sleeping I supposed, and perhaps I too should sleep. Would I still be a tree in the morning? What kind of tree was I: did I have beautiful foliage?

I dozed, the shapes and shadows around me moved and swayed as I drifted off. Then a bright flicker of light in the distance aroused me and attracted my attention. Was it the sun breaking through? Could it be day already; had I slept through a whole night? The brightness grew rapidly and was coming directly towards me, like a train, or motor car. What was a vehicle of that kind doing here, amongst the trees? The brightness neared and the noise accompanying it, a noise that turned to a roar as it grew in magnitude and strength. With horror I realised what it was. A forest fire. I turned to run, but could not; a tree cannot run. I smelled the acrid scent of burning and watched in horror as trees were engulfed and consumed; as the circle of fire quickly widened, the whole landscape was soon ablaze and daylight had arrived — although it was still night. I saw huge trees toppled. Through the burning, creatures of all kinds came running in fear and panic. Badgers, squirrels, rats and even deer ran towards me and I called to them, but they ignored me and rushed past without a glance. Birds circling around, undecided which direction to take were overcome by the heat and the smoke and dropped downwards into the inferno below. The fire was very close to me now, and I could sense the pain of burning even though no flames had yet reached me. So this is what it was to be a tree. A safe, solid citizen, incapable of flight, at the mercy of any attacker and without the ability to defend. The heat was so intense now that I found it difficult to concentrate and I hoped that I would pass out before the fire reached me and I would be saved some of the pain. This was to be my destruction. I could hear, or thought I could hear, the cries of burning trees and animals. The flames

EFAD-3

were so bright they created a special darkness. Nothing new was visible and light and dark had become the same, indistinguishable. The ground was burning, I was burning, everything was burning; I fell forward into the fire.

A piercing cry of an anguished bird that had lost its home rent the air and I looked up into a sky that was grey, haggard and unsmiling. Around me nothing was standing in any direction. I lifted my hand, opened it, and grey ash fluttered down.

Sixteen

My head was throbbing again. Not a constant pain, but a reminder pain that would recur every time I thought it had gone for good. I needed water to splash on my face to cool me down, but I had not seen any for days and I dare not use the precious drops left in my canteen, in case I could not find any for an even longer period. As the blanket of despair was really starting to sweep over me, I saw it — a vast stretch of sea with a flat sandy beach just ahead of me. Only the slope of the hills had prevented my seeing it before, but as soon as I reached this brow I was almost walking directly into it. I stripped off my clothes, dived in and was happily splashing around when I saw a whale. At first I thought it was a shark and tried to swim back to the shore before it attacked. But I was not fast enough, it started to nose alongside and I could almost feel its teeth sinking in before I saw it spout water and realised what it was. I was reassured, but still wary, although it seemed preoccupied and paid little attention to me. I swam away to observe it, as it headed straight for the beach. It came into the shallow waters and allowed the power of the waves to thrust it slowly forward until it became stranded on the sands. I did not understand this, and then I saw that from further out several other whales were heading inshore, coming straight towards the beached whale. Soon there was a line of some ten whales stranded and immobile, with no obvious way of getting back. It was as if by allowing themselves to be beached they were deliberately choosing to die.

I swam ashore and went over to them. They looked at me with gentle eyes. Why? Why? There was no response, just a look of sadness as if that were enough to explain. I gripped hold of one around its tail and attempted to drag it backwards into the water. Its weight was immense and it was almost impossible to hold on to the slippery rubbery surface. I was able to move it perhaps a few inches, mostly sideways but that was of no use and the effort was utterly exhausting. It was very hot, and the whales were soon suffering from the heat and the lack of moisture. I knew their skins would start to blister in the intense heat. I tried to scrape away the sand from under one in an effort to make a slope down which I could push it, but it was impossible to do this, the sand was soft and the whale only settled even more deeply into the depression I was creating. There were large shells on the beach in which I carried water to splash over the whales to give them some relief. They seemed to understand and their expressions indicated their thanks but relief was only momentary. I had no idea what else I could do but did not want to leave them to die. I was depressed at my inability to do more. I roamed the shore and the rocks trying to find assistance. Hoping to chance upon a way of providing help but there was none. Perhaps the only thing to do was to save them from further agony and help them to die. It did not seem possible to kill a whale without causing it further pain and agony, and then becoming in some way responsible for its death. I did think of burying them in the sand to suffocate but that would be a very slow process and they were still likely to die in agony. Perhaps a rock to strike them, but if I did not kill them outright they would suffer greatly and again I would be the cause of pain and become part of their final agony.

I could not abandon them so decided I must share their pain and wait for them to die. I sat some fifty yards away from them, my place in the sun, my eyes fixed on them. Mainly they were still and silent but occasionally their tails twitched and their bodies wriggled.

It was a long and heavy day and I was long and heavy with guilt, suffering as they were, as the sun fiercely bore down and dried us out. Then the evening was upon us and with it the darkness came quite quickly, and I then lost sight of them as the blackness of night conquered. There was no moon and no stars to give light but although I could not see them I could imagine their vast, sad shapes lying there, motionless, awaiting death.

It was a night of bitter tears and I sat with my head down, my imagination running riot, the suffering of the whales like massive weights on my shoulders. I do not remember falling asleep but occasionally I must have done.

My head ached and my eyes were thrust forward from their sockets. I was worn out, emotionally drained, exhausted.

The morning light filtered through and the greyness crept away. I had not the strength or the inclination to raise my head to see those fine creatures in their death throes, but eventually I stood upright and stared at the place where they had been. They were not there. The sands were empty, there was not even an impression left by the huge weight of their bodies. Mysteriously, during the night, they had vanished. How could that be?

Seventeen

The lake or sea stretched forever. At least it seemed so. As far as my eyes could see to the left and right and straight ahead. It might be an ocean but there was a smudge of something on the horizon in the far distance which indicated land perhaps, or the pointing finger of a peninsula corralled by this vast crocodile green water. Possibly there were crocodiles in it. Possibly that's why it was so green, it was really a mass of crocodiles from end to end. Just a wild and idle thought.

I picked up stones and threw them in different directions and watched them sink, the ripples spreading outwards until they met and disintegrated in confusion. Nothing stirred, no crocodile snapped its jaws, and nothing responded to my actions. Without knowing why I decided to cross to the other side. I was not a good enough swimmer to attempt that distance, and looked for some assistance. There was certainly no boat to hand, nor should there be. It looked as if I would have to attempt to walk all the way round. I walked a few yards while I puzzled it over, but still was at a loss what to do. If only I could fly. Stranger things had happened to me so perhaps I could. I raised my arms and tried to flap them and to imagine myself soaring upwards but remained utterly landlocked. I could build a raft. I would look for anything suitable although I had no idea how I would fasten the wood together if I found any I could use. There was a dense clump of trees nearby and I made my way towards it. The trees formed some kind of circle. They were more or less evenly spaced but were so solidly rooted there was no way that I could either pull them down or topple them over. I wrestled with one for a while but only tired my arms and felt rather foolish cuddling a tree in such a clumsy fashion. A whimsical looking squirrel sat across from me in one of the trees watching my efforts in total amazement. "If I had teeth like you, maybe I could gnaw away at the bottom. Perhaps I could bribe you with some nuts." I was talking to myself, for the branch was suddenly empty, the squirrel had moved on to more interesting sights. Perhaps he had gone to fetch me some tame beavers! I was thinking foolishly I knew, but otherwise I did not have any prospects of finding something to help me get across the lake. Then it was there, as if conjured up by my very frustration or imagination. Hidden within the trees, a disused wooden building had fallen into disrepair. Shaped like a hut, but with gaping holes where storms and winds had tried to pull it apart, it was obviously without an owner, just waiting to be used by me in a new capacity. It already leaned precariously and it did not take much for me to topple it completely. I broke off parts until it ceased to look like a disused hut. One wall which was more or less complete I could definitely use as a raft. It was much heavier than it looked, and I started to drag it slowly through the trees to the shore. Half way there I realised I would need oars to steer it. I went back and took two more pieces of timber which were about the right length and shape. Sometimes I pulled, and sometimes I pushed, eventually getting them to the water's edge. It was a raft all right, and it floated, although I had one moment of near panic as it almost floated off, but I managed to grab it and beach it until I got myself ready. I put my pack at the front with one fairly flat stone at the back to provide counter weight and then took the two pieces of wood to use as oars. My trousers were already so wet that it did not matter about getting them wetter when I edged the raft forward from the shore and scrambled aboard.

I waited for the current to move it out, but in fact it did the opposite and the craft slumped backwards against the shore. I had to keep using the oars to push off, and gradually the boat gained some momentum and started to float out. It was taking me in the right direction so I did not bother to row but merely enjoyed the sensation of the gently rocking water. Sometimes it splashed over the whole of the raft but it did not matter as the wood was quite solid and there was no way it could sink. After a while I became quite bold, even standing upright, feeling quite the captain of the ship. The water was clear and I could see the long shadows of water plants waving graciously at me as I passed over them. Eventually the water deepened and blackened blotting out the sight of what was beneath. The water being mainly calm, with just the occasional ripple, I made slow progress but I did not mind.

Without warning the raft rocked and I almost lost my balance. Then it was still again, only to be rocked once more, this time even more violently. I saw a strange looking claw gripping the far side of the raft pulling at it, rocking violently. With one of the oars I pushed at the claw which gripped it tearing it forcibly from my grasp and tossing it away. The raft was then subjected to a series of violent shakes and considerable rocking. The pack was slipping off, and I threw myself forward to catch it and hold it down. The other oar and the stone had already gone and now the raft had one end just below the water with the other sticking up in the air. I was frightened to move towards that end to balance it in case I lost my hold on the pack and it might fall overboard. The claw was still fixed to the side of the raft then it moved slowly forward, toppled over and fell sideways towards me, I saw that it was not attached to anything and presumably had broken off from some creature. It did not appear as if this had happened recently or that it had any life of its own. I just could not understand how it had attacked the raft in that fashion. I touched it gingerly, half expecting it to jump up but it was totally lifeless. I wanted to throw it overboard but was afraid that in some way that might re-activate it, so I decided to leave it in the middle of the raft, turned away from me. I was now without oars, unable to direct the raft which drifted onwards under its own momentum, moving further away from the shore I had left and closer to the other side. At one point the raft hit an eddy which spun it quickly around, while I gripped the sides in case I fell off. The boat spun six or seven times more, before it broke free and drifted away. I felt that I must be in the middle of the lake as I could faintly see land on all sides but now I had no idea which way to head as I was completely disorientated. The claw had gone, presumably it had been swept off while the raft was turned around but I was not certain of this, its disappearance created an uneasiness which made me apprehensive, and I looked continually at the sides of the raft in case the claw tried to attack once again. I could not see beneath the inky black impenetrable surface of the water. Sometimes I sensed movements as if creatures were swimming alongside and I wondered if the crocodiles I had imagined earlier were in fact now all around. One end of the raft was still an inch or two in the air so I edged myself further into the middle in order to keep it more evenly balanced.

There was a knocking on the wood beneath me. Three knocks — silence — again three knocks. I waited for a few moments but there was nothing else. Then I knocked on the boards and from below came an answering three knocks. For one brave moment I thought of climbing off and trying to swim underneath to see what was there but the blackness of the water made me too scared to try, I might lose contact with the raft and then be totally lost.

A bird, apparently exhausted from some long flight flapped downwards and perched on one end to rest. Three more knocks on the wood and the bird took off in fright, flying weakly, barely a foot above the water; I hoped it would make it. I turned my attention back to the raft and when I looked again the bird had gone from sight. After that there was no more knocking and though I knocked at intervals there was no reply.

The water cleared and I could see the raft was surrounded by fish swimming alongside, so close I could reach out and almost touch them. Sometimes I dipped my fingers into the water but they just glided around my hand without any fear of being molested, treating it as some minor obstruction.

One moment the water was pleasant and cool, my hand trailing in it, the next it became boiling hot, all around fish were dying. I tried to withdraw my hand but it was as if some magnetic power was forcing it to remain submerged and I could not remove it. The pain was so intense that I started to lose consciousness and lay on the raft, my hand still held in the burning water which was now so fierce it had started to steam. The raft bumped ashore and I was woken up and could feel the water had become cool once again. However, I had no feeling in my hand, and withdrawing it slowly from the water I held it up to look at it. It was no longer a hand and resembled the claw which previously had attacked the raft and then fallen lifeless onto it. I stumbled from the raft into the water and waded through the hundreds of dead fish floating to the shore.

Scores of rats were running down to the water's edge seizing a fish and running off with it. It was a horrifying sight. I attempted to drive them away, but there were too many and they ignored me, darting between my legs and continuing to seize the fish. I struck at them with my claw, hitting a number. Immediately, as if by some signal they ceased their current activity and turned their attention upon me. They were in their thousands, and their violent red eyes gleamed viciously at me. I was terrified and started to run away from them up the beach. Sensing victory they ran fiercely after me. They were at my heels, nicking at my feet and legs almost tripping me, and I was fearful I would fall and be swarmed upon. I reached a tree, with a despairing leap I tried with all my effort to take hold of an overhanging branch; a hand could not grip it but the claw could and it held fast, I could then pull myself up and scramble on top of the branch. The claw had stuck. I pulled at it to try and free it but it would not move, then it detached itself and simply fell off onto the rats beneath. One picked it up and ran off with it back to the shore, the others followed it, leaving me alone.

Almost unconscious with exhaustion, fear and pain, I lost my hold and balance, and fell from the tree to land at its base. As my mind was passing into oblivion I heard three knocks.

The Head

It was a heavy, wet, oppressive day. Not raining but feeling as if it were. It was the kind of day to forget. I had to keep walking and I kept my feet firmly on the ground and my eyes on them, looking just far enough ahead not to trip over. A few yards on I saw a round object sticking out of the ground which, at first glance, looked very much like the shape of a head. Then I realised it was a mound of earth shaped like a head, but when I came close to it, it was in fact a head — a head that was alive — a head with a mouth which spoke. "Hallo," it said. An innocuous enough word for someone in what can only be described as an incongruous position, but probably it was as good as any other with which to start. At first I did not reply, too surprised by what I was seeing. "Please don't ignore me," the head went on, "I do rather badly need your help."

That was certainly an understatement. Feeling rather foolish, I bent down close. "What are you doing down there?" My enquiry was as absurd as asking the man going down for the third time if he was drowning. Therefore without waiting for a reply, I continued, "I'll help you get out. Just let me find a stick or stone to start digging with."

"Thank you very much," the head said with an apparent smile. It was rather difficult to decide its expression as it was covered in earth and grass which is why I had originally thought that it was just a mound of earth and why I might have passed it by had I not been keeping my eyes down. Well there was something to be said for a bad day.

I found a flat stone that I could reasonably grip and started to dig away at the ground around the head. I had to dig very carefully so as not to harm the head, which I now realised belonged to a man, but I could not help tiny bits of dirt getting into his eyes, and every so often I would stop and clean them away as gently as I could. The head did not complain, taking it all with very good grace. It certainly seemed a very nice head. As I made progress, I realised there was a lot more to this head than I had anticipated, it was the head of a very large man indeed. As I uncovered them the naked shoulders were revealed as being extremely muscular. Perhaps I should have guessed from the size of the neck that it was part of a very well-built body, but I had not really thought about it until I saw the shoulders appear.

Gradually the arms also came free, and then he was no longer a head, but half a man, and naked. I wondered if the whole of the man was naked, but somehow it was an impertinent or possibly irrelevant question to ask at that time, and anyhow I would soon find out. I was trying to be extra careful now with my digging. The man's arms were totally free and he stretched them above his head. He became quite excited as he knew that his freedom was imminent.

I was almost exhausted from all my efforts and said, "I'll have a short rest now. I'll go on again in a moment." The head's face darkened, his arms quickly swept downwards and forwards tightly gripping mine. "Don't stop! You can't leave me now, I've been like this too long. You must keep digging!"

I was shocked by this response and tried to pull away but his fingers, vice-like in their intensity, held me fast. "Don't worry," I said, "I will set you free, but I must rest a little. Calm yourself."

But the head's eyes had a strange look, and he would not loosen his vicious grip. "No," he said. "I will hold on to your left arm while you dig with your right, then you can't run off and leave me." I said nothing, but my face became set and I kept my eyes down, continuing to dig with the right hand as he had ordered. It was an uncomfortable position and my right arm ached incessantly. It was very slow and difficult going. Accidentally, again some earth was flicked into the head's eyes.

His instinctive reaction was to lift his hands to rub them, thereby releasing my arm and I was able to roll away out of his reach.

"Don't leave me," the voice implored behind me, but I was adamant in my determination to leave. However, I pushed the stone I had been using to within reach of his hands so he would be able to dig himself out. Of course it would take a much longer time for him, and I would be far away before he was free.

"The next time you find a head imprisoned," I told myself, "you must ignore it and keep on walking."

Nineteen

Another day and the curious heat of yesterday had temporarily abated. I wanted to keep up a fast pace in order to reach the range of hills in the distance by nightfall. I still needed to set myself goals otherwise it would have been too easy just to give up.

I did not see the hole. Looking back, I felt almost certain there had not been one to see. But there I was, my feet touching nothing but space, falling downwards into a pit, hitting bottom with a tremendous painful thud. As I lay, dazed, I tried mentally to retrace my steps but still could not work out where the hole had been and why I had not seen it; I could remember only the grass stretching out before me, looking the same in front as it did behind. The hole did not appear to be very deep and I did not expect much difficulty in getting out of it. I sat up and waited until I was more rested and able to make the effort to climb out. I stared at the sky overhead, at least in the hole I would be partly protected from the direct blaze of the sun. I stood up to examine the walls of the pit. Surprisingly they were very smooth and free of any marks, as if made by a machine, not by the hand of man, nor by any random act of nature. Each wall was exactly the same, flat and smooth and without any means of assistance to climb it. There was a branch lying on the floor which I used to try to dig into the surface of one of the walls, but it immediately snapped. I then examined all the surfaces closely, they had a hard stone finish which was impenetrable to any of my efforts. The walls were about twelve feet high. Using my pack as a base to stand on, I tried to scramble to the top, but could not reach the rim, and each time I tried I fell backwards to the floor. Then I crouched in one of the corners, and springing forward tried to sprint the tiny distance across in order to make a leap and try to gain a hold on the edge to pull myself out. On just one occasion I managed to get both hands touching the edge of the hole but the sides were too sheer and there was no way I could pull myself up and out and I had to let go and again fell. I tried several different ways to climb or leap out but each time was unsuccessful until finally, utterly exhausted by my efforts and totally dejected by the lack of success, I lay down to rest in one of the corners.

I really was in a hole, and could not help a wry smile at this feeble joke, as feeble as I felt. I was becoming very alarmed, aware that too many efforts to try to get out would gradually weaken me and that I must not cause any injury to myself. I was already hungry and thirsty, but I knew the more efforts I made to escape the more my hunger and thirst would increase. There was no apparent alternative but to rest and wait to see what other events might happen; there was always the faint hope that eventually someone would pass by. As the sun moved round, my corner of the hole started to heat up, and I shifted my position so as to remain always in shadow as far as possible. It helped slightly although it was still very hot and my mouth was parched. I tried shouting but this was both tiring and weakening and not knowing if anyone was likely to be within earshot it seemed pointless and futile. The shouting had made my throat even dryer and increased my thirst. I realised that unless someone was passing very close by they would not see the hole even from a short distance away, and even then would not necessarily feel the need to look inside. I needed some kind of flag to try to attract attention. I took off my shirt, tied it to the pack which after several attempts I managed to toss upwards so that it balanced precariously on the rim of the hole where my shirt occasionally flapped as the wind took hold of it. The noise of the flapping shirt was somehow comforting.

Several hours passed and I was feeling very low, although

strangely the pains from lack of food and drink had subsided. The shirt flapped suddenly as if a stronger wind had blown up and I heard a noise from one side of the hole. I shouted out. I could hear someone or something moving around, but when no head peered over I fell silent. I realised that I was at the mercy of anyone who wanted to take advantage of my predicament. I thought I could hear a scraping noise and possibly breathing, but was not certain whether this was my imagination or the sound of the wind. Suddenly my pack and shirt were knocked back over the rim of the hole, to land right in front of me with a crash. I did not move and waited to see what would happen next. Other objects were thrown down and I pulled myself back into a corner to avoid being hit. Then I realised that they were some kind of vegetable and after a moment's hesitation I grabbed them and started to wolf them down, not caring whether they were edible or not. In fact they were soft and tasted quite delicious, and I quickly finished them. A larger object was thrown down which ricocheted around. At first it looked like the head of a monkey so I approached it gingerly and picked it up. It was a coconut. I could hear the milk slopping around inside it. There was no obvious way to open it so I smashed it against a wall and as it split open juggled with it so that I was able to retain most of the milk although quite a bit spilt. I drank greedily and then broke off bits of the flesh to suck. Only when I had finished the milk did I suddenly think that I should have saved some in case I needed it later. There were bits of coconut left on the ground, and I picked them up and carefully stored them like precious jewels.

Without warning the sun went down and I was in total blackness. I could not see either the moon or stars and it was so dark that I was not able even to see my own hand. I felt my way round on all fours till I found the pieces of coconut, holding them close in case I needed to guard them from some unknown intruder, but probably more as a means of comfort.

I now began to hear a lot of movement and sounds around

the edge of the hole, and felt that there were faces staring down at me. I somehow imagined that they could see me, even though I could not see them and it felt as if the hole had shrunk so that we could reach out and touch each other. I waved my arms around in every direction but made no contact with anything except the walls which were as firm as ever. I could definitely hear breathing and I tried hard to distinguish whether it was from a human being or from some other creature. Who had thrown me food and the coconut, and why? Had I been trapped here for some special purpose and how would I learn what it was?

I passed an uncomfortable night, dozing occasionally, even falling asleep, but always waking up in alarm after dreaming of strange creatures shuffling around me, and then as I became fully awake realising that it was only the blackness that enveloped me. All the time I strained to identify the sounds of the breathing. Gradually it seemed that the intensity was magnified as if whoever it was out there was trying to get closer to me and from then on I could not allow myself to sleep, but forced myself to stay alert.

The first lines of light started creeping in as morning arrived and as light filtered the blackness the hole became filled with a swaying greyness. My back ached, my legs were stiff, my mouth was very dry. I took a piece of the coconut and nibbled at it. Then with awkward steps I stretched myself within my prison. I could walk from one side to the other in just two strides. The previous day it had taken four strides. I shook myself totally awake as I tried to puzzle this out. The hole definitely looked smaller. It was the same height but the area across was less. I could not see the sides moving but I knew they were. I stood in the middle and stretched out my arms. I could not quite reach either side. Then I could. Soon my fingers had to turn upwards into an upright flat hand. The light completely cleared away the greyness and the pit was brightly lit with no hidden corners. I stared at the walls and tried to see them actually moving but could not. Yet they were. It seemed as if only the wall behind me was moving each time and I would spin around trying to catch a movement. The walls formed a narrow box, my box, my coffin. I wanted to pick a piece of the coconut from the floor, perhaps my last piece ever, but I did not dare bend down in case I was not able to straighten up again. Better to remain upright than be forced on to all fours. The walls pressed in on my shoulders. I could not lift my arms. I could not even turn.

A black bird flying way overhead on its lookout for food suddenly dived down and snatched at a big fat juicy worm that was wriggling in a small hole in the ground. It was a square hole.

Twenty

The rocks were harsh and unrelenting. It had been a sheer climb and the skin of my fingers had been torn in the effort to pull myself upwards. There had been no easy way. I had attempted, and had eventually succeeded, in climbing in an almost vertical line until I was able to crawl over the rim and lie on my back, full of pain and exhaustion, but also with the elation of having managed it. What a godforsaken place I had arrived at. Hardly any vegetation was able to grow here and the ground stared at me stark, austere and unwelcoming. I felt a strange, powerful eeriness which I could not fathom. On my right were stacked a number of loose stones, all curious in shape and design. They were extremely thin, smooth surfaced and sharp edged: almost matching, yet each strangely different. There were no round edges at all, it was as if some ancient fairy-tale giant had with his axe sliced into a block of stone rendering it into equal sections, and had then cut into each one at random. I looked at them and they were important to me.

I imagined there had been some volcanic history in the area, although those stones did not appear to have any volcanic qualities. The atmosphere was exceedingly dry. It was as if no rain had ever fallen. The ground was arid and scorched to a lifeless dark brown. As I started to recover I half raised myself and noticed a series of small narrow crevices in the ground, just beyond and to the left of the cut stones. At first I thought they were not in any regular pattern, just haphazard zig-zags. Then as I got up and studied them more closely I could see that in fact they did form a pattern of sorts, a system of parallel lines that stopped and reformed a few yards further on. I peered down them but they seemed to go on for ever and I could discern nothing, only a blackness that alternately seemed both to threaten and beckon me into itself. I was pleased the crevices were too narrow for me to slip into because each time I looked down I felt a dizziness that tried to suck me into the depths below. I wanted to estimate how deep the crevices were so I took one of the loose cut stones ready to drop it in to hear how long it took to hit bottom.

Holding it in my hands, I felt how incredibly smooth it was and yet it was just a stone. Although very fine and narrow it would not pass through the first crevice I tried, then I found one into which it fitted perfectly, and for a brief moment the crevice was no more until the stone slipped gently and silently through. I suddenly realised that the shape of each stone matched one of the crevices. I selected the next stone and matched it to a crevice and again after a moment's hesitation it too slipped through and went down without a sound. I then took them all in turn, slipping them one by one down the appropriate crevice. No sound came and at first it was a disappointing result and I felt rather foolish as if caught doing something childish or silly, but there was nobody there to laugh at me but myself.

I heard the rumble of thunder and looked upward in astonishment at the perfectly clear sky, wondering where the sound was coming from. Perhaps it was from a distant valley which somehow had contrived to bounce the sound all this way. It did not seem very likely. The rumbling in fact was too close and I soon realised that it came from inside the rock itself. The ground beneath my feet was beginning to vibrate and I tried to run away from the edge, but it was too late, it descended in controlled easy movements like some natural elevator operating on its down button.

I was now on a ledge perhaps three feet in width that stretched the whole length of the cliff face and that all the way along was going down at an even pace. At first all that was revealed was a rock face similar in texture to the one on which I was standing but as it descended, a head of enormous size was disclosed staring straight back at me. It was beautifully carved, inlaid with gold and silver and with precious stones for its eyes. As the ledge continued downwards the whole figure of a huge man was revealed.

As I glanced along, I could see there were dozens of these giant figures, each one individually carved and shaped. The ledge slowed, and as it stopped, sank into the rock floor becoming part of it so that I was able to move backwards and stare in awe at the magnificent sculptures that were now fully revealed towering above me. It was like entering a hidden cave of the past and finding giants from another world, petrified for all time until my discovery. Each foot was also huge, practically my height. I started to walk round them. At the back was an opening through which I could enter. I soon discovered the figures were hollow and I climbed a stone staircase built inside the legs and the body, entered the head and peered out through holes near the gems which acted as eyes. All the figures were joined together by tunnels and chambers and I was able to go from one to another examining their marvellous and individual carvings. They were equal to any wonder in the world. I did not want to share them with anyone. The eyes, the heads and the hands were full of jewels and I wanted all of them for myself. I was consumed by the fever of greed. I prised an enormous opal from one face, and then another, then a ruby, and another and then some amethysts. I worked incessantly, and soon had my pockets full of precious gems. I must quickly hide them in case someone should come.

Weighed down by my stolen treasures I hurried, as best I could, down the steps and away from the figures towards a clump of trees where I intended to dig a hole and conceal the gems. Reaching the trees, I briefly glanced back and with horror saw the dreadful holes I had created in the figures. It was as if they were now suffering from some disease which had pock-marked them; I was the disease. They had been robbed of their beauty and were ugly. I had destroyed them. Suddenly the jewels became merely pieces of stone to me. I went back, re-climbed the steps and slowly replaced the gems. Gradually the figures smiled once more. When I had finished I sat in their shadow in peaceful solitude feeling their strength reaching out to me as if in gratitude and friendship. Their secret was mine, to remain with me, and should not be shared. I was not certain how I could protect them and I sat with them all night, as if on guard, waiting for the morning to come. Just before darkness fell the shadows seemed to make them animate as if they were waking and starting to live.

During the night I heard a light pattering sound, accelerating slowly and then felt drops of rain falling. Here in this arid desert where rain never fell, it had started to rain. It was very warm and I did not mind it, allowing it to wash over me where I stayed sitting cross-legged. My legs felt comfortable and I was happy in this position. Then there was a sudden flash of lightning which lit up all the faces in front of me. I could not believe what I thought I had seen. The rain appeared to be melting the figures. It was as if it was washing away their features and shapes, the figures were being turned back into large unsculpted rocks. I tried to rise, somehow to save them, but could not, and with another flash of lightning I saw that what seemed like the stone from the figure directly in front of me was running down in rivulets towards me and had already covered my legs and this was why I was unable to move.

I was forced to remain in this position throughout the night, mostly in darkness, with occasional flashes of lightning which showed me the figures dissolving more and more. The stone stream was continuing towards me and surely must eventually cover me. Somehow it did not matter and I was calm about this fate. Perhaps I deserved it for tampering with these wonderful objects, possibly thus causing their destruction. As the liquid stone reached my mouth I tried to hold my head higher so as to prevent any entering. I was successful for a short while but gradually it built up until I was totally covered. The weight of the stone continued to increase and I toppled over and fell backwards.

I awoke slowly, my head tender from the rock on which it had been resting during the night. Stretching out alongside the cliff face were strange rock formations, each massive and completely individual, towering far above me. They had been strangely sculpted by wind or rain so that each one seemed to have a life and personality of its own and you could read into each shape something special, a part of a face; an eye, nose or occasionally a smile!

Twenty-One

The day had made a decision to be beautiful. Dragonfly where are you? The air was completely clear and there was a softness and a sweetness in it that made me heady with delight. Every flower seemed more alive and aware of itself. The grass was springy underfoot and playfully responded to my touch as if inviting me to be part of the magical scene. Only wisps of small white clouds were visible, the radiant blue of the sky spreading itself rapidly in all directions as if painted by invisible hands over the largest canvas. Far in the distance I could see clusters of tiny villages, sometimes just four or five houses scattered here and there and then separated from the next group by a small wood or a few fields. On a gently rounded hill top, contrasting with the bold greens and blues of the background, was a simple village church, significant, quietly proud.

I let my imagination sweep towards the villages and although they were too far away to be seen, I could visualise the people waking up, starting their day and leaving their houses to set out on a morning's work. One particular group of white and yellow houses nestled around a far hilltop, actually forming a letter E by the symmetry of their positions. Then something strange occurred. At first, I could see only the outlines of the houses and the church steeple which stood like a sentinel on guard. Then the detail of the houses became clearer, the houses getting larger as I stared, and soon I could see actual open windows, curtains flapping, doors and even the handles on the doors. I rubbed my eyes but it was not imagination, the sight remained. It was as if I was hovering over the village, or that my eyes had suddenly gained powerful telescopic abilities which enabled me to see clearly everything that was happening, even though I was some miles away.

A young and pretty woman came out of one of the houses, with a basket of washing that she started to peg on to a washing line. She appeared calm and happy, unconcerned and unaware of anything else, certainly that she was being observed by me. But as I looked I saw that she was also being observed by someone else. Along the side of the house slid a menacing dark shadow, so twisted and tormented in shape, that it appeared to be more beast than man. It was the one thing I could not see clearly, only its outline, and as it continued towards the unsuspecting woman I knew immediately it meant to attack. Then from the shadow an arm stretched out and I saw a knife, the sunlight glinting directly on its blade. As she worked in that peaceful spot, the woman was unaware that a few yards away lurked the wickedness and evil that could end her life.

I wanted to shout but knew my voice would not carry such a distance. In despair I waved my arms frantically, but there was no way that she could see me at this distance. I cursed the sudden gift that had given me the power to encounter such a terrible experience. There was nothing I could do to prevent the attack, and the sight would haunt me forever.

The twisted shape became more definite and growing bolder it crept nearer to the woman's back. The knife was raised, some sense caused her to turn and face her assailant. I saw her mouth open in a scream which reached my heart, if not my ears, she flung her arms outward to the sky and stood silhouetted for one terrible moment, a moment which for me passed into eternity. The grotesque shape plunged forward, fell in front of her dissolving into two; two children had been playing a frightening joke on their mother. She was crying and laughing, they were laughing and crying, but none of them knew that I watched them, crying most of all.

Twenty-Two

The sky was full of colour. Colours that in some strange way were alien and out of place within it; mauves and greens, sepias and every shade of yellow. The air was clear and fresh and I could walk for hours with hardly any effort, just part of the mysterious landscape. I was walking under a stretch of sky which was predominantly primrose yellow, when I heard the music. At first I thought it was a bird whistling its own special tune, but soon realised the music was coming from someone actually playing an instrument. It soon became clear what it was, the mellow and soothing notes filling my ears, and I was drawn towards the sound that I felt could mystically enchant and hypnotise the whole earth within its spell. I wanted to find out who was playing and especially why. As I approached, the high ground fell away, and I had a clear view of the figure of a man sitting cross-legged, his flute poised to his lips, his fingers an extension of the expressive instrument. In front of him, the magical sight; two small mice-like creatures squatted on their hind legs, their front legs held high and straight, with their faces turned towards the flautist, as if mesmerised by the beauty of the music. I was unnoticed, the player played on, neither he nor the two furry creatures paid any attention to me, and I felt moved by their stillness, their complete absorption.

I sat down, a little way off, on a small mound, and also listened. The notes rose and fell with perfect symmetry, and I tried to keep my breath still in order not to interrupt or cause any intervention in the concert that I had chanced upon. Why was the flautist there? I did not know, but for the moment I just enjoyed the magic. He was intense and sharp featured, he wore a black shirt and white trousers, and he was barefoot and hatless. At the end of each piece, the sounds would die away, and the silence would become unreal, and almost unbearable. I wanted to applaud, but was frightened to announce my presence so boldly. If only Dragonfly were here with me to share this magical experience, and I could then see again her eyes shining with excitement. What a smile she would give and how she would have loved these tiny creatures.

During these moments of silence the flautist would contemplate what to play next, then he would recommence. Each piece was even more enchanting than before, and I felt myself drawn deeper and deeper into each melody, part of an atmosphere so rarified that my breath was almost taken away. All the time the little mice creatures sat back, still and attentive, never moving or turning their heads, full of the same wonderment I was feeling. The flautist played for at least an hour and then abruptly stopped. He stood up, and produced from his pockets two bags. One long and thin into which he slid the flute; there was a cord attached, and he hung it over his shoulders like a quiver. The other bag was smaller and made of soft velvet material. He picked up the two creatures, and dropped them in one by one, and in amazement I realised that they were not real. Inanimate, they were the perfect audience; they would not applaud, or interrupt, only listen.

The musician put the smaller bag in his pocket, looked once in my direction, but through me as if I were not there, and then turned on his heel and walked away and out of sight. I remained spellbound for a few brief moments, uncertain what to do, then I shook myself free of the spell, forced myself back into reality, my reality at least, and started to chase after him. I followed down into the hollow where he had gone, but there was no one there. There was no sign of him, or any indication where he had gone, or which way to follow. I went back to the spot where he had been playing, and in the dust were the imprints of the tiny clawed hind feet of the two creatures. Also almost covered by the dust, there was a tiny piece of apple. I picked it up, and saw bitten into it a tiny but perfect set of mice teethmarks. The sounds of the flute still lingered, and it was some time before I could shake them clear from my ears.

Twenty-Three

I could not have felt lower. The pain in my head had started playing up again, and I could feel its throbbing louder than my own footsteps. How could I go on? If only Dragonfly were still with me, to inspire me, to give me courage. How could we have parted! I must find her. Perhaps she needed me. I needed her. Where could I look, where could I even start to look? Then as if she had never left I saw her. Dragonfly!

One moment she was nowhere to be seen, the next moment she was walking slowly towards me across the sands, one foot hesitantly in front of the other, her head slightly down, but her eyes up, searching for me. They found me but she did not immediately respond, neither did I. She did not quicken her step but made straight for me. I was silent, unable to move, waiting for her. I studied her anxiously as she approached, but she did not seem to be harmed, just very downcast and lonely. I wanted to reach out to her and cuddle her but my arms did not move. She came up to me, it had been some time since I had realised how small she really was, child-like in body and face except for her eyes which carried a long history; so many years that even she was unaware of their whole story. It was she who reached out to me, crouching at my feet, pulling her arms around my knees so tightly that I almost toppled as her hunched body pressed forward. I thought she might be crying, but when she looked up there were no tears, but the lines at the side of her nose had deepened. If the tears came the river beds were ready.

My own river beds started to fill up and as they overflowed small shining silver trout leapt outwards and over the head of Dragonfly to fall to the ground, their tiny bodies palpitating as they gasped for air. Then the water flowing down formed an arc, picking them up, and carrying them away to the distant lake. I had not realised I was weeping, but the stream of water continued until all the fish had reached safety. Dragonfly looked up at me again, and the waters ceased, except for two single drops which gently floated down and reached her eyes and made them sparkle.

She rose to her feet, I picked up my pack, put my arm around her shoulder and we walked off to follow the water trail down to the lake. We walked slowly and silently, and I never questioned her.

The Lesson

I awoke inside a church. At least, the shell of a church, unused
and empty, grey stone walls stretching upwards to a roof that
was still partially intact, some windows broken or missing. I
closed my eyes, and kept them shut for a minute or two, and
when I opened them the church had vanished and I was out in
the open, but as I looked upwards I saw the clouds scurrying
away carrying some of the stained glass windows which had
remained unbroken within the church.

Dragonfly was still asleep, but as I stood over her, her eyes
opened, she was immediately awake and stood up. I stroked
the tangles out of her hair, and gave her some water in which
to wash. Her dress was looking pretty rumpled, and I thought
about getting her some more clothes.

However, she needed more from life than clothes. She
smiled sweetly at me as she waited for my next thoughts to
come through. "I think today we will have some lessons."
Although I knew she could not understand what the words
meant she immediately sat down, cross-legged, looked up at me
and waited patiently for me to begin.

How to begin? What do you say to someone who has no
knowledge of your civilisation, a girl without background, who
could not or would not speak, and could not understand the
words you spoke. A leaf floated down, I caught it, held it
and showed it to her. She looked at it, and I wondered if she
saw what I did. I asked her "Do you see what I see?" She
looked at me without comprehending my question, knowing
only that I had asked her something. "Yes, it is a leaf," I
continued, "but until a few moments ago it was part of life
itself. It lived and breathed, and had blood, the tree's blood."
I traced the veins with my finger, and she saw the network of

inter-connecting canals. "Now it is cut off from that life source, and will shortly die, but at the moment it is still alive." I let her feel the texture, and I rubbed it gently against her cheek. She responded, caressing it gently, understanding its beauty, its magic, and yet its fraility. She held it up in the air, and let it go, slowly it spiralled to the ground, but before it reached the ground, she caught it again, holding it high and allowing it once more to catch the wind. This time it evaded her, dancing over and above her head as she went forward to catch it. She twirled around excitedly, realising the game that was being played. She followed it as it danced away again, eluding her outstretched fingers. Dragonfly paused and held back, as if uncertain whether to chase it, then another leaf fluttered by, and another, then several more, all joining in the dance, and soon she had no idea which was the original and which had come after. They dipped and swirled, before slowly coming to rest, the wind dropped and the leaves were quiet, silent, waiting. Dragonfly turned back towards me, I beckoned her over, and she sat down once again looking up at me. Picking up two stones from the ground, one polished and smooth, the other rough and jagged, I let her hold one in either hand to feel the strange shape and texture, the great difference between the two. "These are two stones, and although we refer to both of them as stones, see how individual each is, there is no way you could say one stone is anything like the other." She studied them, then putting them in the same hand, she covered them with the other hand, shook them, and then put her hands behind her back. I understood what she wanted, and tapped her left shoulder, she gave me the jagged stone. In her right hand was the smooth one which she stroked before stroking her own face, then she pointed at the jagged stone and pointed at me laughing silently, yet with such merriment that I had to join in.

Taking a thin stick I started to trace in the earth. I drew an aeroplane and was surprised that this was still so much on my mind that it was the first thing that I etched. When I had finished, Dragonfly seized the stick from me, and quickly drew a large cross through the plane as if to obliterate it. Then with a few lines she drew the outline of a running horse, larger than the aeroplane, and more beautiful. Finally she added a large flowing tail which moved, sweeping away my drawing of the aeroplane, and I was very glad.

Dragonfly indicated that I should remain seated while she went to hunt in the grass. Shortly she returned with a tiny beetle which she held in the palm of her hand. Each time it tried to escape she would gently ease it back to the centre of her hand; eventually it became tired of trying, remaining dormant and passive and ready to be observed. She held it close to my eyes, so that I could see the delicate markings on its back, zig-zag and circular lines that spread right to the very perimeter of its tiny shell. Very gently she slipped it over on to its back, and I could see its many legs kicking in the air in slow motion. Its soft under belly was dark and wrinkled, yet of great beauty. When she saw that she had moved me, she gently replaced it in the grass, where it started to scurry away. It stopped, as if to say thank you, and then continued and was gone.

We spent a great deal of time flat on our stomachs, crawling through the grasses, examining insects, stones, and all kinds of magical and exciting things. I hope that we did not alarm too many of the creatures of the undergrowth, perhaps they were pleased that we had invaded their kingdom to learn, happy to be observed, they certainly did not seem afraid. These were very exciting moments, each of us in turn finding something beautiful or intriguing to show the other. Some creatures were obviously very shy, running away at our approach, we heard many strange rustlings and hurried movements as we crawled along.

Tired out, we lay on our backs to rest. My eyes started to close, and the church descended from the clouds to cover me. I hoped it was covering Dragonfly too.

Twenty-Five

I was giving Dragonfly lessons every morning before we set off on our travels. We would start with language teaching, but the rest of the time dealt with anything. Often I would describe famous battles from history, which was always great fun, sometimes piling stones and rocks to represent the opposing forces, then explaining how the attacks began, and how each would try to encircle the other, until at last one had been defeated. If we were near water, I would dig a ditch and put in pieces of wood to represent the flotilla of ships and line them up against each other, and show how the ships were sunk. Dragonfly would enter into the spirit of these games with great excitement, although I guessed she was thinking I was describing a recent battle of her world or even mine. It did not matter and she still gained in knowledge and interest.

Language lessons were more difficult. Because she could not speak, I could never really be certain if she had learnt the meaning of the words I was using. I tried to test her afterwards but sometimes she would react in such an extraordinary manner that it seemed unlikely she had grasped what I had been trying to get over to her. I began by using words that were fairly obvious to explain, like left and forward, and she soon learnt to respond to these, and even more quickly to take up the opposing words. I would pronounce the word carefully, and she would try to mouth it, all the time watching my lips and trying to form the same shape and emit the same sound. Her brow always furrowed as she concentrated on what I was saying. Then I would send her ahead and shout out the new word, hoping she would turn and respond to it in the way I had taught her. I longed for her to speak, and often thought that at last a sound was going to come, but it never did. I could not tell why she did not speak, whether it was shock from a previous experience, or whether she had been injured in an accident, or perhaps tortured. Once, when I had been feeling particularly frustrated in trying to get over my meaning to her, I had tried to examine her mouth, but she quickly shied away and the violence of her reaction stopped me from making any further attempt to learn the reason for her silence. Eventually she developed a good understanding of vocabulary, and I was able to talk to her all the time, feeling she more or less knew what I was saying. I was convinced that she understood or sensed my moods and thoughts, many times she was able to show an incredible perception through her absolute awareness of me. I knew I had become everything to her, but sometimes this great dependence overwhelmed me, I felt so totally responsible, afraid she would not survive without me. I never wanted to part from her, never lose her, but knew that one day there must be an end to this journey. Many times when I awoke she too would wake up instantly, getting up as I did. I wondered if she were terrified that I would leave her, one day waking to find me gone, but I hoped she knew me better than that and it was merely that any of my movements created an immediate response in her. Once I slipped down a gully and struck my head, almost falling into unconsciousness and although hidden from her view, she immediately returned and came straight back and found me. We were locked into the same wave-lengths of thought and response. We were twin souls.

In return for my lessons Dragonfly taught me many things. She knew the land; what berries to eat, what plants and vegetables were not poisonous, how to obtain juice from certain trees, plants, or the strange fruits that grew on the plateaux and hillsides over which we passed. We always carried water, but used it sparingly, in case we could not reach another river or lake for some time, and I followed her instructions on when to fill up from whatever source we came across as we travelled. She knew which antidotes to use when one of us became sick and we always carried various berries, roots and plants she had gathered, she knowing how to use them to alleviate fever or weakness. I wanted to catalogue them in case I ever got back and was able to pass on this knowledge, but had nothing on which to write. I stored certain leaves, berries and seeds, and hoped that my memory would recall which were which, and how each was to be used. Although I usually led the way sometimes she would pull me in another direction, and invariably I found that she had taken an easier route, or had brought us to water, or a special site. That was how we discovered the plateau of the bees. I had been making towards some high peaked mountains, intending to climb them but she had tugged at my arm, imploring me to go around them. I had not wanted to, but her insistence overcame my reluctance, and I was persuaded. As we rounded the side slopes, I was amazed to see stretching out before us a valley swarming with bees. They were of immense size, bulbous and very brightly coloured. Dragonfly pulled me forward, I tried to hold back, thinking we would be stung, and that from bees of such size, the sting would be fatal. But Dragonfly stooped down, picked up some white berries that grew close to the ground, squeezed them open and rubbed the juice on her face, arms and legs, and when I did the same, the bees kept away. Every tree had its own gigantic hive swinging from it, and Dragonfly quite fearlessly collected the honey from a number of them and we had a wonderful feast. It was very thick, not too sweet, delicious and very satisfying.

We spent two days walking among the bees, never once were we stung or attacked. At night we collected more white berries, positioning them around us so that we were protected at all times. When we had passed through the valley, I looked back, it was quite impossible to see it, so hidden was it by the multitude of bees that swarmed over it. When we had climbed high enough, I could see that one stream of bees was moving continuously out of one corner of the valley, and another stream was returning, obviously following a route by which they could gather the essential pollen.

Dragonfly was excited that she had found the valley to show me. She danced ahead, stopping every so often to glance back, giving me a capricious look. Dragonfly was no bee. She was a somebody.

Twenty-Six

The stone is God's own antique; fashioned by wind, sand and water, but most of all by time. I spend a great deal of time playing with stones; collecting them, placing them in appropriate groupings and using them to form faces, expressions, or to create stories. Today I was sitting behind some large rocks, with a whole range of different stones I had collected over the last few days trying to see how they related one to another; what textures and hidden markings lay under the layers of earth that I was earnestly washing away. To anyone observing me, I would have looked eccentric to say the least, but there was only Dragonfly to pay attention, and she was used to my ways, and no longer thought it strange, or certainly did not appear to.

Sometimes she would help me by bringing a stone she thought was interesting to add to my current collection; although I always took it from her, secretly I did not want her to find them, as the pleasure was in discovering my own stones, and invariably I would discard hers later.

Dragonfly was not around at the time, as she had seen me settling down, and had wandered off on pursuits of her own, occasionally reappearing to assure me that she was all right. I would see the top of her head pop out from behind one of the rocks, or even not see it, but feel her presence or shadow, and then she would be gone again. One of the stones was particularly encrusted with hard earth, pieces of shell and other smaller stones, and I had to use my knife to dig away to clean them off. I pushed in the tip of the knife to about half an inch and was levering away when suddenly the tip jammed against something, and the knife sprang back deeply cutting into my thumb. The stone broke in two at the same time, and fell as I dropped the knife and grabbed at the wound. The blood flowed out and fell everywhere.

Inside the stone was a small yellow and black striped bead; forgetting the cut for a moment I tried to pick it up. It was not a bead but a live insect which jumped from my fingers and on to the blood on my thumb, and I felt a fierce stinging pain run through my hand and up my arm. I sprang to my feet, and tried to knock the insect away. I must have done so as I then could not see it. I took a cloth to wrap round my thumb to try to staunch the flow of blood. I felt weak, probably from the loss of blood and the sting, so I sat on the ground again. Then my eyes were covered with thousands of yellow and black striped insects, and my head fell backwards under their weight and was forced to the ground. I tried to raise myself but the weight on my eyes was too great, my head felt swollen to gigantic proportions, and my feet seemed to have swollen too, their weight pinning my legs to the ground. I tried to call for Dragonfly, but my tongue had also expanded to fill the whole of my mouth, so that I could scarcely breathe, and I felt myself choking. I gasped for relief and it came suddenly, and I remember the pleasure of falling asleep or losing consciousness. When I awoke, the insects had gone from my eyes, my head and feet felt less swollen, and my tongue was nearly back to its normal size, but still I could not raise myself. Dragonfly was bending over me anxiously, wide-eyed with fear, she was wiping a wet cloth over my face, the water trickled down under my chin and behind my ears. I tried to smile, but had no control over my expression, and was only able to flutter my eyelids in response. I hoped she understood.

There was no such thing as time. I existed. Dragonfly would be there and then she wasn't. Sometimes I thought she was when she was not, and other times she did not seem to be, but I still felt the water trickling behind my ears. It would be light, then dark, and I could not tell if it were a day passing followed by a night, or if my eyes were playing tricks. Sometimes light was followed by dark and then by light again so quickly that I could not believe a whole night had passed by, but mostly I just did not care what it was, or where I was, or what was happening. I don't remember eating, but I do remember the water trickling, sometimes into my mouth, out of my mouth and down my neck, and always behind my ears. I must have had the cleanest ears of anyone, and I wanted to share that joke with Dragonfly, but could not express it, and then could not remember why it was funny, and then what it was anyhow.

At times I felt very cold, and Dragonfly would cover me with all our clothes, and used I think to pile stones around me to try and keep me warm. At other times I would become so hot that my whole body started to burn up, and I wanted her to take everything off me, even the clothes I was wearing, but she did not, and eventually I would forget, and float away.

I could not see anything except Dragonfly's eyes, they were always big, anguished and full of fear. I wanted to comfort her, but could not, sometimes the water she used to wash my face came straight from her saucer-like eyes in a direct stream that fused us into one. Some of the water trickling into my mouth tasted salty but very sweet, and although I hated to see her cry, they were the times that I felt most refreshed.

Gradually I became aware of more light than dark, and I seemed to see the sun floating in a yellow mist, revolving around the sky, my eyes able to follow its rolling movements. I became aware of the hard ground beneath, and of aches in my arms and legs and the stiffness in my neck. I managed to smile. Dragonfly's tears ceased half way down from her face to mine, then rolled upwards and vanished, as she mirrored back a weak smile.

She fed and washed me. I started to drink more thirstily, and more went down the inside, and less ran away down the outside of my face. I was able to sit up, Dragonfly holding me and supporting me until I could keep my body upright without toppling over. I remembered my thumb but there was no pain.

My mind and voice returned, and I was able to speak. "How long?" I asked. She held up one hand, fingers outstretched, and then held up a second in a delicate latticework pattern. I was amazed. "Ten days" I exclaimed, and she nodded.

I had lost part of my life, spending it half-crazed in delirium, but at least it had only been ten days. I wondered how many people had died during that ten day period. I hoped the black and yellow insect had gained an extra ten days of life in exchange for the ones I had lost, but I doubted it.

I got to my feet unsteadily. Dragonfly looked up at me, happy to relinquish the role of leader, allowing the decisions to be mine again. "Let's go on," I said, and we did.

Colours

This time she had awakened first. I knew that because I awoke feeling drops of water on my face and found her gently washing my eyes and stroking my face into wakefulness. My eyes opened, but I did not stop her, and she continued for a few moments more. She had laid out some food and sat cross-legged watching me eat it, refusing to take any herself. She usually ate little, perhaps because of long periods of starvation she did not need much food or possibly she was terrified to allow herself to rely on it in case there came another time when she would be without. Soon I was on my feet, ready, and she waited for my first move. I strode off briskly, she trying to maintain the same speed, never lagging behind, even if at times she seemed to be running to match my stride. I felt like taking her hand, but held back as I was still anxious not to create too much dependency knowing that one day there might have to be a parting. The road became very rocky, then fell away to a deep decline and it was difficult for me to maintain a footing without stumbling or using a hand to steady myself. Dragonfly did not need this as she was so sure-footed she was able to leap from stone to stone in a steeper downward movement than I could ever attempt. She never let herself get too far ahead of me, always pausing so I could come up to her before she continued. She was still the slim creature I had first found, but now there was colour in her skin, and lights in her eyes, and her hair had grown longer and bounced softly around her head.

As we descended a mist filled the valley ahead and we could not see through it. At first it was grey, then blue and then in parts green but as we entered still further it almost instantly became a deep crimson. The mist was thick, fog-like, strange and eerie to move through. For a moment I lost sight of Dragonfly and shouted for her, thinking that we might become separated and lose each other. But she had had the same thought and came back through the red mist to stand anxiously at my side.

Now I did take her hand, not out of affection, but of necessity so that we could keep in contact and this slowed our descent. The mist swirled about us, colouring everything with a redness so that no other colour was visible. I looked at Dragonfly and her head and hair had become red. So had her clothes and body, even her eyes looked like two bright red coals. I looked down at my own arms and legs and realised that I also had become completely red. I rubbed at my clothes and my hands but could not remove the colour, it was as if we had been sprayed with a dye and were coloured into this red world. I wondered if we should breathe the air, and if we were poisoning ourselves. I thought of trying to fight our way upwards out of the mist. But as I looked up it seemed even thicker than below so I decided it was preferable to go on in the hope it would soon clear. Dragonfly seemed very anxious but would go where I went. In fact the mist was becoming thinner now, and seemed to be clearing and I could see further ahead. The bottom of the valley was not too far away. There was a river with a line of trees on either side that partly obscured it. The water was red as were the trees and despite the thinness of the mist everything was still red coloured. Dragonfly suddenly pulled her hand away from mine, almost causing me to overbalance, and I thought that she was falling, but she moved to one side and was staring at something on one of the rocks. I followed her slowly and cautiously and saw that what it was, was coloured green. Why would it be green if everything else was red? It was definitely bright green. It was green and dead. A beetle lay on its back with its legs completely immobile, although not quite straight, as if having given a final kick against the blanket of death that had covered it. We were puzzled, then we saw a green butterfly, it too was dead. Dragonfly gently prodded at the beetle and the butterfly but nothing happened. Then we saw a green badger — also dead. The eyes which stared sightlessly out onto a red world were green, all its markings had vanished into a greenness which vividly contrasted with the red shapes and contours of the rocks and stones around it.

Now we were nearly at the bottom, still holding hands, although we hardly needed to as we could see more clearly. As Dragonfly moved ahead our arms became outstretched, and I pulled her back with a suddenness that shocked her into my world of fear.

She followed my gaze, looking at her arm and it was slowly becoming green. She held out the other one and that too was turning green. I pulled her towards me but she snatched herself away, obviously thinking faster than me, and started to run away. She did not want me to touch her as she realised that green represented death and I still had red arms. I paused for a moment to look in case they had started to change but their colour remained as before, then quickly I dashed after her. She was faster than me, and would have got away but in my haste I lost my footing and stumbled and then fell several feet at once and crashed into her and then together we crashed further down until we reached a level area. I gripped her firmly and would not let her go. Her arms and legs were completely green. Anxiously, I stared at her, uncertain, I could see a greenish tinge in her face. She was becoming rigid like the dead creatures and for a moment I thought she was going to lie on her back and thrust her arms and legs into the air but instead she rolled herself into a ball as if to blot out the sight of her own metamorphosis. I curled myself around her trying somehow to force my redness over her to blot out the spreading green but with no effect.

I do not really know what made me try it but it seemed like the only thing to do. I picked her up and ran the last few yards through the trees, the red trees to the river, the red river, and dipped her into it. The only way I could do this was by immersing myself as well and the water covered us totally for a few moments. As I pulled her to the bank I laughed and screamed and shouted, and she thought I had gone crazy until she saw what I had seen, and she gripped me tightly, not being able to scream and laugh and shout out loud. The green colour had vanished and she was as red as before. We splashed about in the water pushing each other down, drenched and soaked through, but not caring as long as we remained this beautiful, wonderful, magical, life-giving red. Eventually exhausted, we crawled out again and lay there very wet but very happy. I tried to look up the valley to the top but could not see through the red mist which acted like a blanket slung between the mountains to close in the valley and its river.

Exhausted, we slept a short time, and whilst I slept I saw a green dragon roaring towards me, exhaling huge clouds of green smoke that destroyed everything in its path, withering plants, and killing off the butterflies, bees, and birds it encountered. Just as it came up to me and the green smoke started to reach me, I forced myself awake, bathed in sweat, and looked round anxiously for Dragonfly. Perhaps she had coloured green again whilst I slept, and I cursed myself for not keeping guard. Dragonfly was sleeping peacefully, and there was no green anywhere. I did not want us to stay there any longer, and I gently woke her. She sat up at first with the same panicked and startled eyes that I had had, and I wondered if she had dreamed the same as I had and seen the green dragon. She could not tell me, but was obviously glad to get up and leave with me. It took us some hours to walk along the valley floor and find a way out between the mountains. We found a passageway, squeezed through it, and without noticing exactly when it happened, found we were no longer red, but as we had been before. We kept walking and climbing until we could look back down and into the valley we had left. It looked an ordinary valley full of ordinary mist, coloured blues and greys. But we knew that it was still there waiting, and we were happy to have left it behind us.

Twenty-Eight

There were five of them, lithe, muscled, with glistening skins. Five youths, surely they would help us! They were laughing and playfully wrestling with each other and I saw no reason why Dragonfly and I should have anything to fear from them. I led her out from the passageway behind the rocks and headed towards them and the hills beyond. They seemed to pay no attention to our approach and again I felt reassured. Then one of them tried to strike a passing butterfly with his hand and I felt apprehension. Another picked up a stone and threw it fiercely at a rabbit which squatted some distance away, in safety it thought, then I felt fear. They were not there to help us! We continued walking, but were no longer relaxed, Dragonfly moving closer to me for reassurance. I could feel she was tense and nervous and ready to react in a moment. I saw that the five were studiously ignoring us, but were in fact as much aware of us as we of them. I altered our course slightly, not obviously, so that we would not approach too close, and for a moment I thought that this would work. Then the five, casually but as if with a pre-arranged plan, also shifted their positions so that again they were directly in our path. Again I altered direction, Dragonfly responding to my slight touch, but the five nonchalantly reacted, starting to edge towards us. I wanted to run, but doubted if I could out-distance them. Although Dragonfly could probably run even faster, I knew they were more likely to go after her, and I could not risk that. I had to meet the confrontation calmly and seemingly without fear, I slowed down our pace, and almost accidentally the group of two and the group of five became a group of seven. Everyone was smiling at everyone else, but they were smiles without warmth, smiles of aggression on the part of the muscular young men, and smiles of fear on the part of myself and Dragonfly.

One stuck out a hand in greeting, still smiling, and unwillingly, smiling in return I took it to shake. I was pulled forward and stumbled before I was able to release my hand, and the others laughed. I was no longer smiling, and although I did not look at Dragonfly, as if to try and keep her out of the proceedings, I knew the forced smile had also vanished from her face. I waited for their next approach, but they seemed quite happy to run around us, chattering in their native tongue, laughing at their own jokes, and allowing the uncertainty of the moment to work for them, reducing my will to resist, draining away my strength. Firmly I took Dragonfly by the hand, almost marching her away to the hills, breaking through the cordon of glistening bodies. Individually I was bigger than they were, but their size came from their grouping, and they did not feel threatened by me. They began touching me, but not Dragonfly, just lightly, and then flicking their hands away. If I tried to respond to one, another would dart forward to prod me or push me or just tap me. Humiliated, I felt I had to ignore them, and I continued to hurry Dragonfly away, not running but as fast as I dared so that we could cover the ground quickly.

Perhaps for the first time I became really aware that Dragonfly was female. Only a girl-child to me, but to them very much a girl. I was sweating and I tried to control it, as I knew the beads of perspiration gave added strength to our tormentors. One pulled at my arm in a provocative fashion, I lost my balance, and nearly fell. As I righted myself I saw two of them pulling at Dragonfly who, unable to speak, was screaming only by opening her eyes and mouth as wide as possible. I rushed at them, they quickly released her and spun away out of reach. Another struck me in the back which caused me to reel into Dragonfly, the collision winding us and causing us to stop. I had a knife in the pack, but was frightened to bring it out as it would escalate the conflict between us, and if they should get it away from me, or if they had knives of their own, Dragonfly and I would be in great danger.

We continued this way for a time, pressured, taunted, punched and pulled, fear draining away our resolve and reserves of strength, but each time I pulled myself together, knowing that Dragonfly was totally dependent upon me, and would not be able to help herself in any way. We were then at the foot of the hills, and we started to climb, hoping to be left alone, that our attackers would remain on the plateau and not bother to climb after us. But they did. In fact they were more agile than I was, and were able to scramble around and above us, increasing their torments by rolling small stones down to impede our progress. I constantly changed direction to avoid them, but they were easily able to catch us, I could not shake them off. Dragonfly was just a shadow of herself alongside me, and although she was able to scramble more easily over the rocks than I, she was now doing it totally mechanically, emotionally withdrawn and rigid in her fear of what was to come. I climbed between rocks, and down passageways and anything else which would give us shelter from the increasing boldness of their attacks, but there was little that I could do to prevent their mastery of the situation, and their confident swaggering approaches. I was constantly pummelled, touched and pushed, and they were more familiar with Dragonfly, her humiliation doubling mine.

I knew we could not go on much longer. I was very tired and my legs were weakening, but I did not dare stop or sit down to rest. That would be the end. They would make a final attack and take Dragonfly away. They probably had plans for me as well. I fought my way through another crevice in the rocks, and heard them laughing and chattering behind. I pulled Dragonfly with me, and then saw why their laughter had increased. In front of us the rock face fell away into a deep chasm, the sides so steep that we would never be able to climb down, it felt as if we were on the edge of the world. There was only one way across, a small rope bridge stretching precariously from one side to the other, swaying dangerously in the wind.

With delight they waited to see what I could do, sensing my fear, knowing that they were in total control. If I attempted to cross the bridge, I would need both hands, and would not be able to protect Dragonfly. However, if we started to cross they could untie or loosen the ropes, and that would send the two of us hurtling down. For a moment despair made me so giddy that I almost swayed over the edge, but I felt Dragonfly's anxious hand steady me, and I shook my head clear. Her strained face implored me to tell her what to do, I knew that if I had said hold my hand and let's jump together, she would have done so without question. I knew what I must do. I pointed to the bridge and pushed her forward, feeling her resistance at leaving me, I pushed her again and this time she ran on, starting to cross. The laughter of the youths ceased, as they realised that at least one of their victims was escaping. They edged towards me, closing in. Summoning my strength to resist I was able to gain sufficient time for Dragonfly almost to cross. One of them pushed at me again, and I moved back under the pressure, as if about to fall. Sensing victory, the boy pushed at me again, so that I almost fell on to the rope. Another push. This time I pulled upwards, and taking the outstretched arm twisted it and pulled the attacker on to my body, encircling his neck with my other arm, dragging him backwards across the swaying bridge. The others could not intervene, as the way was too narrow, and I slowly backed across the bridge, the boy struggling in my arms, my grip on his neck never loosening, so that his struggles were in vain. The rest could not decide what to do. To kill me they would have to kill one of their own, and that was unacceptable. It was a long journey backwards, and I could not grip the side ropes to assist me, more than once I stumbled, almost falling, the rope swaying precariously under the weight of two bodies. The boy in my grasp was now petrified and realising that his own life was literally in my hands, he ceased to struggle, and allowed himself to be dragged, now praying for my success. I sensed Dragonfly's eyes on me, trying to guide my footsteps. I could feel her reaching out trying to strengthen me, and it helped. Then I felt her hands touching and guiding me, she had been unable to stand it any longer, and had run back along the ropes and was now my eyes and balance.

We reached the other side, and I released the hostage, who collapsed and almost fell over the edge from exhaustion. I pulled him to safety and sat him upright. He sat there with imploring eyes, wondering if I would do to him what he and his four comrades had planned for us. I almost wanted to, and certainly felt that some revenge was called for. Dragonfly, as if reading my thoughts, touched my arm and my anger drained away in response. I could see the others on the far side, watching, angry and thwarted, waiting for their chance again. I knew they would pursue us, and I could not allow that to happen. I sent my captive back along the rope walkway. He was reluctant to go because he feared my intentions, likening them to his own. I forced him, and he had no choice. He started off slowly and fearfully, and then as he gained distance, his bravado returned, and he looked round shaking his fist and yelling his threats. I did not respond, but took out my knife, and started to cut through the ropes. The bravado vanished. The boy started whimpering, struggling for the other side. I went on cutting, until there was only one main strand holding the bridge, it was now swinging backwards and forwards in great dipping movements. I waited until the terrified figure had reached the end, and was being pulled up by his friends, then I cut through the remaining strand, and the bridge plummeted and caught by the wind twisted and turned until it crashed against the far side of the chasm. Dragonfly and I were safe.

Exit-But-One

When we first saw it, we had no idea it was an island. Certainly not the usual kind of an island, surrounded by water. There wasn't any water. Only a broad expanse of land that stretched for many miles from where we stood until it reached the shrouded conical plateau that rose dramatically upwards. This didn't appear to be a mountain. The plateau was foreign to its surroundings. As far as I could make out from this distance it was densely wooded and covered in thick vegetation; a place wild and mysterious, powerful and majestic. We decided to cross to it over the land, flat and yielding, which although not actually wet, had that softness that riverbanks get when they have been drained. I did not puzzle about it too much then as my eyes were set firmly on the strange area ahead I was eager to reach. Our going was slow, as the softness caused our feet to sink down, it was even further than I had estimated, and took us most of the day to cross the vast expanse of nothingness. Immediately we reached it we began to climb, but the day and ourselves were exhausted, and it became dark quite early. The best thing was to rest, camp near the bottom of the slopes, and start our main climb the next morning. Dragonfly was quick to agree, and within a few moments of stretching out in a small gully, she was fast asleep, and I soon followed.

I was awakened by something lightly patting me on the face. It was so soft that it did not startle me, and I slowly opened my eyes and looked upwards, and felt more drops of rain. I woke up quickly, as did Dragonfly, and we took shelter beneath a large beech tree that gave plenty of protection. The strength of the rain increased, and soon it was falling at an alarming rate. The water had the power of a monsoon, and soon broke through the branches of our tree, making us wet through.

We decided to climb a bit further on and then we found a cave in the hillside easily large enough for the two of us, and we lay there watching and hearing the rain pounding into the ground around us. It would not stop, Dragonfly and I were imprisoned.

We were in a cave full of cobwebs. They hung in profusion from the ceiling, down to the floor, from every projection that abutted the cave walls, sometimes so thick they gave the impression of being embroidered curtains put together by human hands, rather than finely drawn webs spun by spiders. Some of them must have been there for years, and as we brushed through them they fell on top of us, breaking into thousands of pieces of dust, joining the dust of other webs that thickly covered the floor. The older webs were certainly uninhabited now, and had long since been abandoned, but possibly the ghosts of ancient spiders still roamed through them, waiting for the ghosts of their old prey to re-enact the waltz of death they had danced so many aeons ago.

Deeper into the cave we found fresher webs, and as we broke through these, heard the tiny sound of the spiders dropping to the floor and scurrying away. I could feel them crawling on me, even though they were not. I shouldered my way through the gloom to where an eerie light penetrated so that we could just see our way, the swaying strands floating around us. The way cleared, although the dust remained thick under foot. I anticipated it by a split second, looked upwards to see a large web falling down as if to envelop us. It was the web of truth.

The intensity of the rain continued, there was just a blinding sheet of water cascading in front of the cave so we could not see through it, but we could hear and feel the storm as it cut off almost all the light and powered its way downwards. We retreated deeper into the cave, waiting for the rain to stop; a long wait, a long time, it continued non-stop for several days. We had food with us, and eked it out, patiently, waiting. The force of the rain was always to be felt, the cave walls and ceiling vibrating and reverberating from its strength.

Suddenly it stopped, as if someone had just turned off a tap. The air cleared, and at the entrance of the cave we could see the sunlight breaking through. Gradually we ventured out, our feet sinking down in the mud as we laboriously took each step. Dragonfly was the first to see what had happened. She flung out her arms in total amazement, and we saw that the land we had passed over was now covered in water, and that the area to which we had climbed was indeed an island, surrounded by water which had come up the side of the hill to where we were. A deep lake had been formed around us, as if it had always been there, although we knew it had not been there when we crossed over.

We explored the island, it was fascinating, with wonderful things to observe; giant plants, and exotic flowers that we had never seen before, exciting small, woodland creatures that bustled and rushed around squeaking in great excitement, trying not to be seen. Tall ferns and grasses, bushes with violet and mauve coloured leaves, multi-coloured exotic birds flying and swooping high overhead. Sometimes the trees were so thickly intertwined there was no way we could penetrate through them, and when the wind blew we could see sparkles of light like a thousand stars creating their own framework emitting light and shadow on the ground beneath. Mostly the silence was so enormous we were intimidated by it, and then a loud echo of sound would burst through as a flock of birds rose from the water giving great whoops of joy before vanishing into the undergrowth or into far away trees. There were elegant roses, bright reds, magnificent yellows, stormy blues, tranquil whites, and fierce brooding blacks. Everywhere rose petals lay in giant heaps in front of us, creating strange shapes that had life of their own. There was power here.

Surprisingly, there was little to eat on the island, mostly berries, and one or two root vegetables, and beautiful as it was, I knew we could not stay very long, and would have to move on.

There was, however, plenty of water from the lake, and on

the topmost part of the island I discovered a spring, crystal clear, constantly bubbling and giving off a shower of sweet translucent white water. We preferred to drink this to any other water, and each morning we would make a pilgrimage together to the spring in order to drink there. We made our base further away lower down in a natural bower that was created by a grouping of trees within some rocks, this giving us protection from the wind, as well as providing a secure place to sleep at night. Although there seemed no reason for fear, our past experiences made us cautious.

Each morning we rose very early to explore the island as well as watch the sunlight breaking over the horizon, gradually stealing across the water, reaching the island, lighting up everything in its path. Sometimes we tried to find the last patch of darkness so we could race the sun as it moved across.

I was feeling particularly tired this day, and put my head down for a moment. I slept deeply, without dreams, and then was as suddenly awake. I felt cold, and wondered if the rains were coming back again, but the sunlight was still sparkling. Then I saw the snake, enormous, luminous, swaying with its deadly precision slowly towards me. Its vivid, clearly defined markings were amazing and I was able to admire them quite objectively as I wondered whether to move suddenly or to ease myself away. I did not shout for Dragonfly, in case she too was endangered. My objectivity soon vanished as the realisation quickly came that I was trapped and could not escape, as if either I was still asleep, or the snake had hypnotically pinned me to the ground. It was going to bite, and I would die, and there was nothing I could do about it.

I tried to remain calm, but felt bitter indeed that such a thing would happen now after all we had gone through, and I agonised as to what Dragonfly would do without me. The snake slid further forward, started to pull itself up to its full height, its tongue flicking out impatiently, ready to make its strike, and then reared for its attack. As it did Dragonfly threw herself in front of me, and at the same time the spell I was under was broken, and I grasped a heavy stone and brought it down upon the snake's head, crushing it instantly into lifelessness. But it was too late, and I knew it. The snake had struck Dragonfly instead of me. Her eyes were open but she was motionless, and I gently turned her sideways, finding the marks of the fangs that had bitten right through her dress and deep into her skin. The skin around the marks was rapidly turning blue, there was no way that I could cut it without helping death on its way. I made her as comfortable as possible, and quickly rushed into the woods, and brought her any berries I could find, in case any of these could be used as an antidote. She shook her head, and we both knew time was running out. The snake was lying nearby, crushed, lifeless, but still frightening in its death mask. I had one last quixotic idea. I started a fire, poured water into one of the pots, and then threw the snake in and boiled it. The water emitted noxious fumes, becoming a dark brown concoction, quite evil in appearance. Dragonfly was deathly white and listless, taking no notice of what I was doing; she was sinking fast. I poured some of the foul liquid into a container, and forcing her mouth open, poured the liquid in, she tried to resist, but at least some went down. At first she became very still, and I thought she had died. My heart seemed to stop, I was going to die with her, but within a few moments her breathing became easier, and she fell into a deep sleep. I could not take my eyes off her for a moment in case, while I did the breathing stopped. She remained like this for that evening, that night, and for most of the next day. Then she opened her eyes, and I knew my strange actions had been right. But she looked and was very weak, and needed nourishing food, particularly meat, and this could not be found here on the island. I knew I must get her away, or else leave myself, to find food to bring back. I explored places we had not been to before, but only bringing back berries, or fruit that I could find. The last place to try was the water line itself, and I set out to walk around the island completely. Magically, it seemed, almost half way round, I came across a derelict cottage, within it, upturned as if once used as a table, a narrow, very weather-beaten boat. It was still a boat, perhaps it could be used. Under the boat was an even more amazing find, a double-barrelled shotgun, with two cartridges, the gun wrapped in oilskins to protect it. There were no other cartridges, only the two in the gun. I made my way back to Dragonfly, dragging the boat with me and showed her the two objects I had discovered. She was pleased about the boat, but terrified at the sight of the gun. Every time she saw it her body shook, and I had no choice but to hide it from her. I had always known she hated weapons of any kind, allowing me to use my knife only for the simplest things, never to hunt with, and she would have never allowed me to use the gun. However, I knew if I could I would use it without telling her, so I could feed her something more than berries, and I considered shooting a bird, and debated about it for days. I did not know how I would explain it to her, but hoped to find a way.

The throbbing in my head had returned with a vengeance. Each day it became worse. I tried never to let Dragonfly know I was in pain. She asked for water from the spring, and I set off to bring it. I took the gun with me. As I approached, for the first time I saw an animal drinking from it. It was a magnificent antelope, massive horns, and with a glistening and bright mottled red coat. At this moment I could not really appreciate its beauty, all I could think of was the chance to bring some real food to Dragonfly, and without considering the possible consequences further, I raised the gun and fired. The antelope leapt upwards, then somersaulted down into the undergrowth.

The shot reverberated all around, and the birds unused to such a sound took flight and for a moment the sky was darkened by their panic flying. I felt panicked by the shot myself, and rushed towards the spring. As I approached, I saw the spring had ceased, and when I arrived, there was not a trickle of water left. I felt as if I had shot the spring itself, rather than the antelope, and that the spring had died. I could not find the body of the antelope anywhere, and in my longing to find food for Dragonfly thought I must have imagined it.

I realised I had been away too long, and rushed back through the undergrowth. Dragonfly was lying there with her face turned away, and when I walked around her, and lifted her face, it was covered in tears. I knew why she was crying, for she had drawn in the ground the outline of the antelope, and she knew what I had done. After that she grew even more listless, what little strength she had fast ebbing away, and I knew I had to get her away from the island very quickly. I carried her in my arms, she weighed no more than a leaf, and carefully laid her in the boat and made it ready. I put in water, berries and vegetables, but was frightened to overload it, as it hardly seemed capable of carrying her weight, let alone mine. I had patched it up as best I could. Slowly I started to row, although I did not know in which direction to head. I rowed at a gentle pace, frightened to upset the boat. My arms soon tired, but my heart forced me on, and within a short time I had left the island far behind, and was heading out into the open sea. Dragonfly lay at the bottom of the boat; her eyes mostly closed, although occasionally and with great difficulty she would open them and look at me, everything we had experienced together contained within those glances. I would stop every so often and give her some water, and soon she could not swallow any of the berries, only the water could trickle down her throat; I took none myself, saving it for her. I kept rowing, expecting this to be our last journey together, the final journey.

My strength gave out, and I could row no more. I lay down in the boat, beside her, so that I could see her face, and hold the water container in my hands, occasionally to moisten her mouth. She knew I was not taking any myself, and tried to motion it towards me, but did not have the strength to insist. I knew that I would not take any as long as she was alive and there was still a chance. The sun beat down, and it became unbearably hot in the boat, and I tried to shield her with my hands. I could not tell even if the boat was moving. I tried not to fall asleep, because sleep was too easy, and I knew we would be robbed whilst we slept. Robbed of life. My eyes shut, I forced them open again, soon they shut again, and this time remained shut.

Exit

The report in the paper was brief, and as easy to miss or overlook, as Exit himself had been in his life, and was even more so near to his death. A Norwegian freighter had picked up a man, or at least what was left of one, in rather strange circumstances. A narrow and battered canoe, virtually on the point of sinking, had been seen drifting, apparently abandoned. Although it contained a small bundle there had been no sign of life and at first the captain did not think it worthwhile to stop and was going to continue without investigation. For some reason he could not fathom he had changed his mind, and they had sent a small boat to tow the canoe in and bring in the bundle. They found that the bundle was the body of a man, huddled within the remnants of his clothing. He was barely alive, dehydrated and suffering from severe burns after long exposure to the sun. He must have been in the canoe for many days, possibly weeks. He had no identification, and nothing in the canoe with which to identify him. His condition was extremely poor and it was not known if he would live.

He lay unconscious, delirious, and even after a number of days the doctors could not bring him back to any kind of consciousness. He was not responding to treatment and could not answer any questions. He only made one sound, uttered one word, which eventually they had been able to comprehend, and it was a word he feverishly repeated over and over. "Dragonfly, Dragonfly, Dragonfly!"

He moved continually and restlessly in the hospital bed, the nurses unsuccessfully trying to calm and make him still. The doctors gave him their constant attention but did not expect him to recover. His delirium had worsened, and he continued to babble except for the one word they understood, that he repeated, again and again, "Dragonfly".

One morning, two nurses came in to change his dressings. After they had finished, through the closed window they saw a delicate hovering dragonfly beating its fragile wings against the pane as if trying to get in. One of its wings was broken. Despairing of achieving its objective, the dragonfly flew away, and therefore did not see one of the nurses cross to open the window. But if it did return, it could now enter.